SILVER FOX'S INTERN DILEMMA

LYDIA HALL

ALSO BY LYDIA HALL

Series: Holiday Hearts

Merry Mix-Up

Series: Off Limits Doctors

Silver Fox's Secret Baby || Silver Fox's Intern Dilemma

Series: Spicy Office Secrets

New Beginnings || Corporate Connection || Caught in the Middle || Faking It For The Boss || Baby Makes Three || The Boss's Secret || My Best Friend's Dad || Corporate Heat

Series: The Wounded Hearts

Ruthless Beast || Merciless Monster || Devilish Prince || Relentless Refuge || Vicious Vows || Lethal Lover || Sinister Savior || Wicked Union

BLURB

He's my mentor. My superior. My forbidden desire.
   And now, the key to my future... or my downfall.

Dr. Jack Thornton: Brilliant surgeon. Devoted father. *Silver fox.*
   I'm just another wide-eyed intern... until our worlds collide.

His little girl steals my heart as quickly as he does.
   Family game nights. Pancake breakfasts. A glimpse of the life I crave.

One heated night changes everything.
   But our passion comes with a price.

Hospital policy forbids us.
   My family demands I leave.
   His ex-wife threatens to take his daughter.

Now I'm carrying a secret that could destroy us both.
   Or create the family we both desperately want.

When love, ambition, and family clash...

Will we find a way to heal our hearts, or will everything fall apart?

★ Indulge in this steamy medical romance! A demanding silver fox doctor, his talented protégée, and the unexpected twist that turns their world upside down. Watch as they navigate professional boundaries, family expectations, and the deepening bonds of love. Available now on Kindle Unlimited! ★

1

SOPHIA

S currying up the hallway after the pair of doctors I'd only just met, I tucked a strand of my straight brown hair around my ear. It'd fallen from the ponytail I had to wear for work because I had to hastily stuff it up in a rubber band upon arriving. My schedule said to be here at eight, but I wasn't informed there would be thirty minutes of prep to get set up for my first day.

Running late and playing catch-up wasn't the best way to make a good impression on my new boss, Dr. Jack Thornton, chief resident of surgery here at Twin Peaks. Five minutes on the actual job and I was already making a fool of myself and feeling intimidated. Meanwhile, Dr. Calvin Briggs, the other intern assigned to Dr. Thornton, seemed smug about having known the routine ahead of time, which wasn't difficult given he was a second-year resident and I had never worked here.

"Try to keep up, Dr. Chen, we don't have all day." Dr. Thornton was stern and serious, and who would expect anything less. He walked so quickly with his long legs that my tiny four-foot-eleven frame could hardly keep up. I felt like I was running a marathon just trying to stay with the men who both towered over me, though Dr.

Thornton had a few inches on Dr. Briggs. I wondered if they always walked this fast or if they were doing it to spite me.

"Sorry, I'm so sorry," I muttered, breathless. I clutched my chart to my chest and flicked the hair out of my eyes again. The damn unruly strand was going to bug me all day. Hopefully, I'd have time at lunch to get a brush and put it up properly. Had I known anyone with long hair had to tie it back properly even on non-surgery days, I'd have done it before I got here. I wanted to make a good impression, not flounder like this.

"So, let's jump right into things. We have a bit to catch up on now that we have a late start." I could've sworn he gave me an evil eye, but I averted my gaze so I didn't have to feel the sting of disappointment.

I did, however, catch the smirk on Dr. Briggs's face and knew he was getting a kick out of this. How much more foolish could I look having been late? I was outnumbered on my team. I had secretly hoped the other intern I was partnered with would be a female, and this was just my luck. Dad's lectures about how I'd be happier somewhere "more prestigious" didn't even begin to touch why I was tense right now.

I stutter-stepped to keep up as Dr. Thornton walked us through the hospital, and I tried to remember every twist and turn. I had to focus on where we were going and how to get back on top of the breakdown of things he planned to discuss with me specifically over the next few weeks. There was self-care and time management, introduction to our clinical workflow, and so many other things.

The longer he talked, the better I felt and the more I settled in. It wasn't any easier to keep up with his long legs, but I managed to scribble some important notes in my notebook. I'd long forgotten where we were and would probably have to ask someone for directions on how to get back to the main office area and doctors' lounge, but at least he'd already forgotten about my being late.

"Alright, first pop quiz of the week," Dr. Thornton said as he turned around. He walked backward, thankfully at a slower pace than he had been walking, and continued talking. "Patient has had surgery

SILVER FOX'S INTERN DILEMMA

on his lung. It's twenty-four hours post-op and he's developed a high fever. What do you think it is? Dr. Chen...?"

He looked at me, and I felt suddenly flustered. My mind went blank when I tried to recall my training and the finals I took only a few months ago. I felt hot, my heart racing, and I shook my head. "Uh... infection," I said hesitantly, and I had so much self-doubt it was impossible for him to not see it. I had to have been as white as a sheet.

"Dr. Chen, you're not a first-year med student. You're a licensed physician. This is your surgical residency. I don't have time for hand holding. What is it?" Dr. Thornton's scowl unnerved me more than I already was. I didn't know what to say. I fumbled for words.

"I, uh." It was like my brain forgot how to think and I couldn't put together a coherent sentence. All my schooling, straight As all the way through and graduating Summa Cum Laude, and I was a real flop. "I guess it could be—"

"Guess? You're saving lives here. You're not paid to guess." He shook his head at me and rolled his eyes in frustration. "Dr. Briggs," he said and looked at my co-intern.

"It's atelectasis. The lungs aren't fully inflating post-op." Dr. Briggs delivered his answer with such confidence it had me rattled. I felt my cheeks warming and my palms sweating.

"Yes, atelectasis is correct. This is basic stuff, people. I shouldn't have to remind you of any of this at all. Now let's get going." He turned and continued walking, drilling off a few more questions as my wounded ego screamed into my ears what a dummy I was.

I tucked the same damn strand of hair behind my ear and dipped my chin so I could make more notes on my notepad. If I learned nothing else in this situation, it was that I needed to study more. He was right. I wasn't being paid to make stupid mistakes and put patients in harm's way. I had to be more on the ball and show how capable I was even when my own self-confidence faltered.

I followed both of them around but stayed quiet for a lot of the morning. It gave me time to reflect on Dr. Thornton and his teaching method and work ethic. He seemed like a very smart man, very confident and self-assured. He was brilliant too. Everything that came out of his mouth was punctuated with importance and value. It was like he didn't let a single word slip off his tongue unless it would teach me something, and though I doubted Dr. Briggs needed to learn any of this stuff, even he seemed to be soaking it in.

Around lunchtime, I was finally able to take a short break and put my hair up correctly. I hid in the ladies' restroom and cried softly about how much I wanted to make a good impression and how badly I'd done at that. Dr. Thornton probably thought I was a fool or at the very least too shy. Dr. Briggs had made faces that led me to believe he thought I was stupid, and even a few nurses gave me the stink eye today.

I was glad I'd taken this internship, though. If I did what my father wanted me to do and I got dropped into some super prestigious hospital with world-class doctors, I'd have been humiliated and probably sent home. Those places wanted the best of the best, and while I knew I was really smart and very capable with medicine and a scalpel, I wasn't the best when it came to one-on-one pressure with a boss or teacher. I never had been. I did better on my own or in crowds, and I was going to find this very challenging.

I was also going to find it challenging to concentrate. No one told me Dr. Thornton was going to be the hottest physician on the hospital roster. It was bad enough to have him as a boss knowing how strict he was and what he expected from his interns, but to have to be around someone so gorgeous and not get flustered was impossible.

A stupid smile stretched across my face and I knew I had to wipe it off. I had to go back out there and do something I'd never done before. I had to act like I wasn't attracted to him at the same time I had to let go of my personal hang-ups about the way people saw me so I could be more confident and ace this job.

I splashed some cold water on my face, tightened my ponytail, picked up my notebook, and headed back into the main hall. One way or another, I'd adjust and get my feet under me, and then I would prove to Briggs and Thornton that I was a force to be reckoned with. I just hoped I could do it without anyone knowing how hot I thought my boss was.

2.

JACK

I t had been an exhausting week. The first week of new intern rotation was always stressful. It was a lot of beginner stuff— coaching them on how busy they'd be and how to care for themselves, showing them the ropes, giving directions to various places on the hospital campus. This time, though, I had a real doozy. If Dr. Chen hadn't been late to rounds on our first day, I still would have felt this way.

Friday evening and I was on call. I stretched my body out on the on-call bed and put my hands beneath my head on the pillow. The room was quiet for now, but I'd be sharing it with two other doctors who were also on call this weekend. The cramped quarters offered a set of bunk beds stacked three high, a kitchenette with a mini fridge, a small dining table, and a desk to work at. The locker room was right next door, though, which didn't help with sleeping, so I always brought ear plugs.

Pushing them into my ears to try to catch some shuteye before someone called me with an emergency surgery, I thought of my new intern and how frustrated I was with her all week. When they assigned me to her and I saw the status of Summa Cum Laude, I figured she'd be an average overachiever with a big mouth and lots of ambition. I saw the ambition part, but her confidence needed work. Why she'd chosen surgical as her residency when she was clearly not ready for this level of pressure was beyond me.

Every time I asked her a question, she hem-hawed around until I was forced to ask Dr. Briggs. He and I had been working together for a year already, and most of this stuff was old hat to him. He didn't need the reminders and she wasn't learning much, but I had no choice. Holding her hand through this week had been so frustrating, I was ready to go question the powers that be and find out why they stuck me with her.

But she was cute. At twenty-eight, she was a late bloomer. Maybe she waited a year or two before doing her med school or maybe she hadn't selected her major soon enough to be considered. It didn't show on her employee file, but it reminded me of myself. I'd gotten a late start too, and after what I went through with my ex, I imagined there were likely some personal situations involved with Dr. Chen's self-doubt.

Whatever it was, she had to work on it or she was going to be left behind. Dr. Briggs had already proven himself to me time and again, and I couldn't very well give a doubtful greenhorn a position in surgery. She had to be more decisive and quicker on her toes. I wasn't sure she was going to make the cut.

I was just starting to doze off peacefully when my phone vibrated. The urge to throw it across the room passed through my mind, but I was better than that. I had to pull it out and make sure it wasn't an emergency, though most of the time, someone would just knock on the door and wake me. This time, however, it wasn't a coworker calling me in for surgery. The call was from my ex-wife and I knew why.

"Yeah," I said after swiping to answer and holding the phone to my ear. Things were bitter between us, but for the sake of our little girl, Leah, I tried to maintain some modicum of self-control around her. They way she decided to do an about-face on our vows and leave me high and dry, all because she felt she deserved more time than my career allowed us to have, still hurt.

"Jack, it's Dana. I'm just calling to remind you that you have Leah this weekend and I'll be out of town. You know I can't just rush back home. I don't have a sitter, and I expect you to—"

"Yeah, yeah. I know, Dana. It's not necessary to lecture me every time I have the weekend." I kept my eyes shut, hoping this would be a quick call and I could go back to sleep easily. Dana had this annoying way of nagging me about how to parent Leah correctly. She was seven years old already, though, and I knew what I was doing.

"Yes, well I know how very little importance you put on family and the fact that your job is always more important. You should probably put a reminder in your phone so you don't forget. I can't miss this trip."

I wondered what sort of trip she was taking that was so important she could miss the weekend with her daughter, but when I had to work late or needed to get a sitter for a work event, Dana flipped out. It was an infuriating double standard that often affected my ability to work when I was needed. I always made time for Leah, and I didn't feel like my job took any more time away from her than any average doctor.

"Is that all?" I asked Dana, who huffed and sounded like she might blow a gasket.

"You don't have to be rude, Jack. I know you're busy. I'm just saying, Leah comes first. You have to spend time with her. You can't just park her with nurses while you work. Do you understand? I'm sick of you shirking your time with her and being late. If you don't grow up and act your age, I'm going to sue for sole custody, and I have a decent shot at winning."

Her nasally voice grated on me. It wasn't the first time she threatened to do this either, and I knew it wouldn't be the last. Dana was always one breath away from filing the suit, and she never did. She had no grounds. I was a great father with a great career and I was an upstanding citizen. She, however, was a drama queen who cried wolf all the time. One of these times, she would regret it.

I opened my eyes and pressed my hand to my forehead. "I always spend time with her when she's with me. You should be thankful that you get to have her all week, every week. We could go back to the judge and revisit that part. I'm supposed to have her three days on, three off, then four days on and four off, remember?" The shared parenting we had worked out three years ago when we got divorced still worked and was still the standing agreement.

I let Dana have Leah during every week, though, because Leah lived right across the street from the school, and by the time I got home from work on weekday evenings, Leah would only have an hour with me before her bedtime at eight p.m. This made sense and in my opinion was what was best for her as a child. It had nothing to do with whether she was safer or happier with Dana.

"Oh, just don't start on me." Dana huffed again, and I pictured her scowl. It wasn't hard to remember, either. Every time Leah got upset with me, she gave me the exact same expression, as if she could mirror her mother's every emotion. She spent too much time with the angry woman, and I wished I could have her full time just to help her grow up in a less hostile home.

"Just be here, got it?" Dana spat, and I closed my eyes again.

"I'll be there. Just have her ready. The less time I have to spend with you, the better." I hung up so I didn't have to hear her nasty, sardonic replies and my life could be a bit calmer. I hated how what once used to be such a peaceful and passionate relationship had become nothing but an angry feud between us almost all the time. I didn't know how life had gone so wrong, and I didn't care to find out, at least not now.

Dana had her chance and she refused to get counseling or be patient with me during my residency. For the final year of our marriage, we hardly spoke. She found a way to engage in classes and activities every evening when I was home, and she and Leah would go out of town to visit her sister on weekends. By the time she filed for divorce, I knew it had been over for eighteen months.

I sighed and shoved my phone back in my pocket, letting my eyes rest now that the call was over, and when I was about to doze off, I heard a knock on the door.

"Dr. Thornton?" I heard, and I knew duty called.

Apparently, sleep was for the weak, but I was no weak man. I got out of bed and put my shoes back on. Someone's world needed saving, and I had to do it.

3

SOPHIA

The radio played one of my favorite songs as I drove, to which I sang along until I had to focus on the traffic. Mom and Dad did this thing every weekend where we had family dinner. For the most part, I enjoyed it. I always had a good time catching up with my little sister, though our older brothers could be annoying and brag a lot. Lately, I'd felt like the odd man out at times.

Andy and Tom were both off to great starts in their careers, a doctor and a lawyer—though Tom's specialty was medical malpractice and would forever stay that way if Dad had his say. The field of medicine was the golden sphere in my father's mind, and I'd been there to observe firsthand how upset my parents got when Tom, the oldest, tried to do something other than become a doctor. It was a mess and there were a lot of hurt feelings, to say the least, and when Tom graduated and passed the bar exam, he relented and decided to focus on the specialty to make amends.

For a while, things were pretty intense. Family dinners involved mostly arguments and Tom defending his own right to choose while Dad told stories of "how things go in the homeland." He immigrated to the States before he met our mother, who was a nurse at the time, but later pursued her doctorate and chose obstetrics. I wondered my entire life how much of that was due to Dad pressuring her.

Overall, however, my family was happy, and I was looking forward to tonight. I hadn't seen Maylin in months. Away at college most of the year, she always made time in the summer and around holidays to visit home. I'd missed her ever since I moved out, but I had to get out. The oppressive way Mom and Dad pushed all four of us to "do better" and "be more influential" just grated on my nerves.

I pulled into the driveway and parked, noticing all five of the family cars already here. Tom's BMW was right behind Mom's Acura in the garage, and Maylin had parked on the street, leaving the spot behind Dad's Range Rover for Andy's Mustang. He was the only one of us who had a "normal" car, which always annoyed Dad. I thought it was cool, though. Better than the EV I drove to conserve gas money and help the environment. Mom and Dad paid for it. I couldn't afford to splurge on that much.

Before I'd even gotten out of the car, I heard the high-pitched squeal of my little sister and saw her come racing out of the front door. Mom and Dad lived in a quiet neighborhood, which never made sense to me considering how loud us four kids were. But the elderly neighbors adored us and lavished us with baked goods and candy and the occasional lemonade on a hot day when we were younger and our parents were away working.

"Soph!" Maylin yanked the door open and practically dragged me out onto the sidewalk, and I left my purse on the passenger seat as she tugged me into her arms.

"May-May, my God, you cut your hair!" Her once very long brown locks had been whacked off to about four inches of hair. I wondered how Mom had reacted to that one.

My Dad, native to China, was probably used to the shorter haircut, but Mom insisted women should have long hair and no makeup, calling it their "crowning glory". It was leftover from her days as a child being raised strictly religious. I was just happy to see Maylin hadn't stripped her beautiful brown hair and colored it some outrageous color. They would have hated that.

"Yeah! I did." She fluffed her hair on the side and posed, making a kissing face at me. "You like?"

"It's so short," I commented and thought of my own long, straight locks. I would never be so bold as to cut my hair off like that, but she looked amazing. "It's cute."

Maylin hooked her arm around mine and pulled me toward the house, and as I walked away, the proximity sensor on my car locked the doors. I was practically dragging my feet to keep up.

"Oh, my gosh, I met this super cute boy in my advanced physiology class and we went on a date, and my God, you never told me how incredible an orgasm felt when you didn't have to do it yourself."

I burst out laughing at her bold honesty. We told each other everything, but at twenty-two, I figured she'd probably keep some of those details to herself now. I was no stranger to a good romp now and then with a guy I was dating, but it'd been a while. It was refreshing to hear her so happy and excited about a new guy, though, after being dumped by her high school sweetheart.

"Yes, well let's not let Mom and Dad know I perverted you." I snickered and followed her through the front door.

The house was tidy like normal, same floral couch, same ugly striped wallpaper. Mom just had to have it after it was featured on that home improvement show she loved so much. The carpet was new, though, but it was so similar to the old cream Berber we'd always had that I hardly noticed.

"Sophia," Dad said as I walked through the front room, but I didn't stop to say hello. It was his typical greeting. He'd just say your name and that was it. It was strange but it was him.

"Baba," I called as we weaved past the hickory credenza into the kitchen through the arched doorway.

Mom stood at the stove with her apron on, stirring a dish she was cooking. The old, ratty strip of fabric had images of antique stovepipes and smokehouses on it. She said it was a gift from her great-grandmother. I said it looked like her great-grandmother wore it. It was so old, but she loved it.

"Oh, hey, girls." Mom smiled at us as we waltzed in and then brought the soup spoon to her mouth and tasted. "You're just in time."

"Oh, Ma." Maylin whined and scowled. "Soup again?"

"May-May, set the table," Mom ordered, and she went to do it immediately. I'd have at least protested first, but May was always the one being Momma's little helper.

I joined Mom at the stove and pecked her on the cheek then hugged her arm and rested my head on her shoulder the way I did when I was younger. She bounced her shoulder a few times in response and put the spoon to my lips, so I slurped the bite and it was delicious.

"Tomato bisque, my favorite." I grinned and decided tonight was going to be a great family meal.

"Help your sister," she said quietly, and I joined Maylin.

When the table was set and the boys came down from wherever they were upstairs, we all sat around the table. We served ourselves and ate in peaceful quiet for a while until Dad started the conversation by bragging about Tom's newest client, a very wealthy and successful plastic surgeon.

I had always wanted to be a doctor, but when Tom spoke about the law, it fascinated me. I could have sat and listened to him tell story after story of winning lawsuits and court battles. He had a passion for it like no other, and it made me get excited about starting my own career. Though, I wouldn't bring that up around this table. Not tonight.

When the conversation shifted to Andrew and how he was starting his own private practice in some remote small town in the mountains west of town, I was relieved they hadn't brought up my new residency. The past four weeks in a row, I'd been hounded about taking one in Baltimore at the famed Johns Hopkins University hospital. Dad knew people. Mom had ties. I had no interest. I wanted to be here near the mountains, and ultimately, I'd have loved to go overseas.

But Mom and Dad had expectations. And given my father's upbringing in such a strict family, I was expected to follow them. Even

Mom couldn't soften Dad's hard edges. His family's culture growing up was so different from the average American family's.

"May-May, how about you?" Tom asked, changing the conversation again.

Malin had such a beautiful smile as she announced, "I'm on the dean's list again." I wasn't surprised at all. She was so smart and capable, the way I had always been. "And I'm taking this quarter's classes remotely so I can be around here more. I miss you guys." She clapped her hands and squealed a few times, which was met with congratulations and a bit of oohing and ahhing.

But when they were done fawning over her accomplishments and her love of family, Mom turned to me. I didn't even have to look at Dad to know his expression was sour, so when I did, it didn't surprise me.

"And have you changed your mind, Sophia? You've done one week of your internship. Surely, you have to see how this hospital doesn't compare at all to what you could be doing." She took a bite of soup then sopped a piece of bread in it and took a bite of that too.

I squirmed a little. It wasn't that I didn't realize the other hospital was far more prestigious or that it would help my career. I just didn't care. I didn't want to compete with the types of students who would be at Johns Hopkins. I was able to. I was definitely smart enough and capable of doing it. I just preferred to stay closer to home, closer to the family they so wildly praised Maylin for honoring. Twin Peaks was a great hospital, and I was lucky to be working for the distinguished Dr. Thornton.

In my eyes, there was no difference, and I would have a great career without that hassle and having to relocate. In their eyes, I was a failure because something else that they deemed "greater" was out there waiting for me. I felt my cheeks warming as I dropped my head and had a bite of soup to procrastinate answering.

"I, uh... I like Twin Peaks. I'm doing well. Dr. Thornton is a great teacher and surgeon." Never mind my being late on the first day, the way he talked down to me, and the way I was always playing catch-up.

My choices were my choices. I shouldn't have to do what they want just because they gave me life.

"Twin Peaks isn't so good." Dad's broken English only reminded me how in his family, if he had chosen something his parents didn't like, he'd have been shamed and guilted until he changed his mind, the way things worked with Tom and law school.

I just didn't see things the way he did, and I hoped someday, they'd change their minds. Until then, I felt like I was on the verge of repeating Tom's mistake, but I didn't feel like I would back down the way he did.

4

JACK

With the incision made, I inserted the laparoscope and fed it toward the lower right abdomen of our patient. Dr. Chen stood opposite me, watching the monitor along with me as I guided the long, narrow camera toward its goal. Our patient presented with acute abdominal pain and high fever and after triage was diagnosed with appendicitis. We, of course, had the joy of removing the infected tissue to treat the patient, and with Dr. Briggs out for the day, I called Dr. Chen in to assist.

"What you're seeing now are the internals, of course. The colon gets sort of pushed up and twisted in places, but the scope will show us what we need to see." I pushed it deeper and navigated it where I needed it until the swollen appendix came into view.

"Wow," Dr. Chen breathed, and I watched her eyebrows rise. "A few more hours and this thing would have ruptured. Our man would've gone septic." She reached for and handed me the diathermy device, and I took it, though I kept my eyes on the screen for all but the brief second I needed to insert it into the second incision we'd made previously.

"He's lucky he came in when he did," I told her as the tip of the tool came into view via the laparoscope's camera readout. The vessels were stubborn and bled a little even as I tried to cauterize them, but I managed to finish without much trouble. When I pulled the tool out, Dr. Chen was there to take it from my hand as I used the laparoscope to resect the appendix which I'd cauterized.

"Dr. Thornton," Dr. Chen said, pointing at the screen with her gloved finger. "The infection has spread there. We need to resect more of the cecum."

Once I used the graspers to slide the swollen, puss-filled appendix back, I saw the reddish area of infection she was talking about. It was a good call, and one I might have missed if I weren't careful. Though, I was always extra cautious during surgical procedures, knowing how sue-happy people were these days.

"Nice call, Chen," I told her. I removed the appendix, careful not to allow it to burst or spread infection, and went back a second time to resect more of the tissue and avoid our patient going septic. When we were finished, I walked her through the few different ways of doing sutures and then showed her my preferred method. With the patient stitched up, we allowed the nurses to apply the dressing and Dr Chen and I stepped out to scrub out of surgery.

She stood next to me at the sink, tearing off her bloody gloves then plunging her hands under the hot water. I was impressed. When I called her in for this surgery, I assumed she'd be hesitant and skittish again. I thought I'd be coaching her through things and she'd probably faint at the sight of blood after these past two weeks of working with her and seeing her be so anxious. But she did so well I probably could have let her do the surgery herself and she'd have done as well or better than Dr. Briggs.

"You know, Dr. Chen, I'm genuinely impressed." I took a sterile towel off the rack to dry my hands and rested my hip on the edge of the scrub sink, watching her finish. She smiled softly and her cheeks flushed light pink, but she said nothing so I continued. "You were very put-together in there. I might have missed that additional infected tissue without your keen eye. Well done."

"Thank you, Dr. Thornton. I'm just doing my job." Her head dipped, and she reached past me to pick up a towel too. For a brief second, she was close enough that I could have smelled her perfume if she'd been wearing any.

How many times had I caught Dr. Briggs wearing cologne on shift, but it was against hospital policy? Dr. Chen's only scent was sterile, like bleach or disinfectant. For some reason, that appealed to me. It was the smell of ethical behavior and commitment. I felt the corner of my mouth turn up a little. I was impressed with her for the first time.

"Why don't you come by my office here in about twenty minutes? I'd like to talk with you a little more in depth." I tossed the towel into the hamper and pulled my mask off and tossed it too. Dr. Chen straightened and dried her hands while looking up at me with a bit of hesitation in her expression. "You're not in trouble," I added to reassure her.

Relief washed over her features and she nodded. "Alright, twenty minutes."

I walked out the door past her and toward my office where we'd do the surgical debrief. It was a habit I picked up while doing my residency with my mentor at the time. We would go over every step of what happened and how we could improve or what we did well. The digital recorder in my pocket picked up every detail of every conversation, though it didn't provide video. I'd thought at times to bring this to the medical board as a means of helping students learn, since this was a teaching hospital, but I hadn't ever gotten around to it yet.

My office wasn't as much an office as it was an old storage room with no windows and only one door tucked on the back side of the doctors' on-call room. When I was made chief resident, they had to clear things out for me to have this space. The surgical head told me all chiefs had their own office space but in order for me to have my own, without sharing, I had to humble myself. I didn't care. It gave me a space to speak privately with my interns and residents about their performance, and that was good enough.

I sat behind my desk, squeezed between a file cabinet and the wall. The small chair I had wasn't ergonomic, nor was it new. It had been scraped from someone else's office as they moved out for a promotion. I was lucky to even have the space, though, so I didn't complain at all. I brought my own laptop since the hospital didn't issue computers to lower-level management like myself, but they did give me the standard-issue tablet for tracking my charts.

When Dr. Chen knocked, I found myself feeling slightly embarrassed by the space. It was clean, but it was tiny, and there was nothing personal in here. I'd been chief resident for more than a year now, but I was so busy working, I never took time to hang pictures or even bring a plant in here. What sort of plant would even survive with no sunlight? The most personal thing I had was a small, framed school portrait from Leah's kindergarten.

"Come in," I called, but I didn't bother standing. I didn't feel like banging my knees on my desk. The door opened and Dr. Chen walked in. Her eyebrows rose a tick, but she was good at hiding her astonishment about the size of my office. "Come on in. Have a seat." I nodded at the single metal and plastic chair situated opposite my small desk, and she nodded once, shutting the door behind herself.

"Wow," she breathed, and I noticed the smirk on her face briefly. "They stuff you in a closet?"

I chuckled, already feeling like she was more relaxed than I'd ever seen her. The rigors of this job were so intense, I didn't blame her for being on edge during work hours. Seeing a new side of her during surgery had opened my eyes to how I had probably missed the real Dr. Chen under all the stress and strain of diagnosing and performing surgeries.

"It's this or the doctors' lounge... I figured this was a bit more private." I leaned forward over the desk with my elbows resting on it and folded my hands together. "Thank you for joining me."

"Yeah, no problem. What do you need to talk about?" Dr. Chen bit her lip nervously, and I saw the first hint of her self-doubt that I'd seen in a few hours. Only twenty minutes ago, she was so confident and self-assured. Now I was beginning to see the anxiety creep back in and I wanted to nip that in the bud. She was so talented and capable, and if I were being honest, much prettier when she was confident.

"Well, first of all, you did a fantastic job. I had my doubts when I called you in, but you outperformed even Dr. Briggs. I see a little of myself in you, how I used to be when I first took my internship." I spoke with my hands as I talked, gesturing for emphasis. She seemed to watch what I was doing, and I wondered if she was listening.

"Thank you," she muttered, and I continued.

"But I'm concerned." I furrowed my brow, not trying to discourage her. I just knew how hesitant she'd shown herself to be and I didn't want her to be put on the spot. I didn't need her up in my office crying her eyes out. "During rounds and lectures, you seem so indecisive—hesitant, even. I wondered if there is something I'm doing that makes you intimidated. Or perhaps you're doubting yourself too much."

I expected her to be overly sensitive and perhaps even defensive, but she smiled sadly and looked down. "You're right. I do have that problem. I tend to get nervous in groups and feel like my opinion or thoughts aren't as good as other people's." She looked back up at me and smiled. "I know I need to work on that. It's just a confidence thing. I'll do better." Her hands stretched out on her knees and she sat with her shoulders squared, but not stiffly.

I was impressed by that as well, how she took my gentle criticism with grace and acknowledged her area of needed growth. And the way she carried herself made me take notice of how attractive she was too, simple beauty without fanfare or pomp. She wore no makeup, had no fancy jewelry or hair clips. It was her simple, dark, straight hair tied back in a ponytail and a clear complexion. I found myself staring and had to shake that off.

"Then I have a solution. I want you to work one-on-one with me until you've gained the full confidence you should have. You're brilliant, and I want to see how much more you can impress me, but I feel like I'm doing you a disservice by lumping you in with Dr. Briggs. Of course, he's going to outshine you a little. He's second year. You just need to get your feet under you, and I can help you.

"Of course, we'd have to do our typical rounds and lectures, and my private tutelage will be more time outside of normal work hours." I raised my eyebrows, waiting for her to respond.

"Yes, I'd love to." She smiled brightly, and I mirrored her expression. Something fluttered in my chest and I felt awkward. Was I being turned on by this woman a decade younger than me? Warmth pooled in my belly and I realized how tense my shoulders suddenly were. My palms were sweaty, and I felt tongue-tied. I wasn't asking her on a date. This was my job, but somehow, it thrilled me that I'd get to spend private time with her.

"Good, we'll start Monday," I told her, beginning to stand. My knee banged on the desk, like it did every time I stood up, and I winced, but I tried to hide it.

Dr. Chen smirked again and looked down, then reached her hand out to me. "I look forward to working with you one on one. I consider this a very high honor."

When I took her hand, it was soft and cool. She had such a light grasp, such smooth fingers uncalloused by manual labor. And her fingers were neatly manicured but had no polish, another indication that she took rules very seriously. I was such a nerd.

"Good." I couldn't manage more than that.

She excused herself, and I thought my tongue was swelling up. I felt like an idiot. I was flustered by a first-year intern with a pretty smile and a confidence issue. This wasn't good at all. So why was I looking forward to beginning our private coaching?

5

SOPHIA

"Laryngoscope," Maylin blurted out, and I closed my eyes.

"It's too simple," I told her, rolling my eyes, but I knew it was one of the words I had to study. Part of my internship was a series of pop quizzes Dr. Thornton brought up at any given time, any day of the week. His job was to make sure I knew my facts inside and out, and while I spent four years in med school studying these very facts, they sometimes slipped my mind when I was under pressure.

After being called into his office for what seemingly was praise, I knew my flubbing up had to end. I couldn't be flustered by how intimidating this whole thing was. Dr. Briggs and his snappy responses that drowned me out weren't the problem. Dr. Thornton was very intimidating, to say the least, but it was my own lack of self-confidence that kept eating me alive. He hit the nail on the head. I needed to start believing in myself.

"Hey, it's one of your cards." Maylin shrugged and pulled the next one up, spouting off the next term, then the next. I nailed every single one of them, and that stack of index cards with medical terms and their definitions was very large. I had amassed it over four years of medical studies and never threw a single one away, except the few that were damaged when I spilled an energy drink on them the night before finals.

"Can we take a break?" I finally asked her after an hour of her grilling me. We sat at a picnic table on hospital campus during my lunch break, which turned out to be two hours today since we didn't have any surgeries scheduled. I'd been doing private mentoring with Dr. Thornton for a few days after evening rounds now, and I still felt like a fool. He was so smart and I felt like a dry sponge.

He wanted to pour his knowledge into me, but I was always doubting myself, thinking how I could have phrased my responses or interactions differently as he was already moving on to a new subject. What I needed wasn't help learning more terms. What I needed was someone to bolster my self-confidence by teaching me how to be human and have a real conversation without getting flustered. He was just so damn intimidating. How was I supposed to interact with that?

"Sure," Maylin sighed. She'd been home for a while now to visit while doing her studies remotely on her computer. She could do her work whenever, but I knew the flash cards we were doing were helping her too. "What do you want to talk about? Maybe that hot doctor-boss of yours." Maylin snickered, and I scowled at her.

It wasn't that I hadn't noticed how good looking Dr. Thornton was. All the female nurses made comments. Some of them called him Dr. Swoon, but I kept my mind focused on work. I wasn't at Twin Peaks to meet a guy. I was there to learn. Dr. Thornton was incredible, though—for his skill and intelligence. The man literally blew me away with how much he knew and what he'd already done in his career.

"I'm not really looking at his looks, May-May. I have a job to do. I have to stay focused on the medicine. This is my career." She'd learn as soon as she got into her residency that there was literally no time for noticing other good-looking doctors or dating. Every second of every day was scheduled, even this lunch. I was skipping my meal to cram and make sure the next pop quiz Thornton threw at me, I did well.

"Oh, come on, Soph. You mean to tell me you haven't even flirted a little? The guy could be on the next cover of *GQ* and you didn't see how hot he is?" She fanned herself and rolled her eyes back as if panting for breath. It was a warm day, but her humor didn't escape me.

"I mean, yeah, he's cute, but I'm supposed to be learning from him. What good will it do if I get all flustered because he's hot and forget my career?" She had a point, though. Dr. Thornton was about the best-looking doctor on staff. Every woman with a pulse knew it. He turned heads and he wasn't shy about it. Though, I knew he stopped short of being that jerk of a man who used his good looks to get things. I'd worked with him enough to know how professional he was.

"You think he's hot too?" She squealed and then she clapped her hands. "Oh, gosh, if he dated me, I'd just eat him up."

I chuckled. Dr. Thornton was at least ten years older than me, and Maylin was years younger than me too. Mom and Dad would flip if I even mentioned liking a guy that old, let alone my boss. If she brought it up, she'd be put in a chastity belt. No questions asked.

"Well, I have to focus on my job. I can't get distracted by every good-looking man. It's important to me to do well." I nodded at the cards.

Maylin scooped them up and started to pull one out, but she got a thoughtful expression. The wind whipped up and blew a strand of her hair in her face and she tossed it with a jerk of her head, then said, "Does he flirt with you? I mean, has he made eyes at you or something?"

I was hardly his type and not even close to his league. "He's a decade older than me. He could probably have any woman he wants. Why would he choose me? And that's besides the fact that he's my boss." I pursed my lips as I stared at the card in her hand, waiting for her to reveal what it said so I could keep studying, but there was a niggling at my conscience. When I was in his office, he acted a little awkward toward me at the end, like he was checking me out.

It was probably nothing, and definitely something I shouldn't have been thinking about, anyway. "Just give me the next card." I told her and scowled.

"Ooh, Sophia likes her boss," she said playfully, and my scowl deepened.

"I don't have time for this." I snatched the cards out of her hand and stuffed them in my messenger bag next to my laptop and the book I was currently reading. "I need to get back." I stood up and slung the bag over my shoulder and pecked her on the head.

"I'm just saying, it would be a good distraction from the self-confidence thing. If you're checking him out, you'll be focusing on how hot he is. Then you'll be able to just answer easily when he quizzes you."

Maylin smirked at me as I rolled my eyes. "See you Sunday," I told her grumpily as I walked away.

I headed back toward the doctors' lounge feeling a little annoyed but letting her thoughts play out in my head. She just got under my skin the way my family always did, but part of what she said made a good point. I was too focused on needing to prove myself at all times, I let that pressure I put on myself get in the way of what I actually knew. If I could distract myself with something else and not pressure myself, I'd do much better. I could just focus on anything and give my brain a break from the obsession of being the best.

I dived back into work, happy to have been chosen by Dr. Thornton to assist him when Dr. Briggs was readily available. I was moving up and that gave me a boost of confidence. I helped him, and everything he asked, I was able to come back with the right response every time, helping him and finishing the surgery with ease.

When we were scrubbing out, Dr. Thornton was talkative, walking through the things we did in surgery and laying them out perfectly. He seemed happy enough with my performance and I was proud of myself too. Nothing could've felt better.

"You really did a great job in there. I'm impressed yet again, Dr. Chen. Well done," he said, reaching for a towel to dry his hands. He handed me one as I turned to him, feeling my heart well and my confidence soar.

Then the worst thing imaginable in my mind happened. He smiled at me broadly and I swore I saw him wink. My belly flipped and flopped, and all I could see was an incredibly stunning creature God created—not my boss, not a skilled surgeon. He was a work of art, chiseled jawline, stunning blue eyes, and worst of all, it made my body feel like an inferno. I got flustered all over again, and this time, it wasn't a lack of self-confidence.

Maylin had gotten in my head. I was aroused. I was attracted to my boss, and I wanted so badly to keep this heat burning.

"Thanks," I mumbled, swallowing hard.

I finally breathed when he walked out of the room saying, "See you in my office," over his shoulder.

What the heck was I even doing?

6

JACK

D r. Chen sat across from me in my tiny office space again for the second time this week. I was continually impressed as we went over the surgical replay. Step by step, she provided me with a breakdown of what we did. She knew it inside and out, as if she'd studied the textbook and memorized the very routine procedure of removing gallstones.

I listened pointedly and praised her when it was appropriate, but I was more interested in studying the sincerity on her face. The genuine passion she had showed through her expression when she got into the discussion. And there was something different about her today. She kept making eye contact with me, hanging on every word I said. I liked it, though it wasn't because it gave me a confidence boost.

I got to look directly into her eyes and see the gold flecks dotting her brown irises. And she spoke with such intensity at times, I found myself being drawn to her, smiling and truly feeling engaged.

"You have so much knowledge, Sophia. How can you be so passionate and confident in the operating theater, then so backward and flustered during rounds and lecture?" My words were a genuine question. As a man who was intrigued by and even slightly attracted to her, I just wanted to know more about her.

Unfortunately, my question struck a nerve. Her cheeks immediately flushed red and she looked down, biting her lip. I watched the blossom of her personality wilt like a desert flower, and she shrugged. Her shoulders drooped. Her posture shrank back, and I got the feeling she was feeling foolish.

"Hey, I didn't mean that in a negative way. Remember, I'm here to help you build that confidence up so you can have the same bold and decisive personality at all times. That's part of my job as a mentor." My fingers itched to reach out and lift her chin up so she'd look at me, which told me I wasn't just saying these things as a mentor. I was crossing a line by letting myself feel what I was feeling—drawn to her, emotionally invested in her...

When she did look up, it looked like she'd been blinking away tears. "I'm sorry," she told me, but an apology wasn't what I wanted. I was interested in getting to the bottom of this, as a man and as her leader.

"I can't help you get over what's going on if you don't just tell me. I realize this might seem a bit forward since I'm your boss, but I'm here to listen if you think talking would help." I sat back in my chair and quickly regretted it. I wasn't able to lounge backward and relax. My chair was smashed up against the far wall and when I leaned, I bumped my head. I was just glad for a second that she was distracted. I felt like an idiot, trying to be cool and looking like a dummy.

"It's just that my parents are both very honorable doctors. Dad is a cardio-thoracic surgeon. Mom is a well-known obstetrician. My brothers both did their residencies at Cambridge in Boston." Her lips turned downward into a pout. "We've lived in Denver my whole life. I didn't want to go out of state for my residency. UC wasn't accepting surgical residents by the time I signed up. They were full, so."

"So you settled for Twin Peaks and your parents aren't pleased?" I asked, realizing there was so much more than a lack of self-confidence going on. Coming from a family of middle-class working parents, I felt the pressure too. Except mine wasn't to be the best to keep the family tradition alive. My pressure stemmed from being the first college graduate after four generations of coal miners and garbage men.

I changed the course of my family history forever, and my gut told me Dr. Chen was afraid of doing the same thing, but for opposite reasons.

"I just have to do well. They hate that I took this particular internship because they don't see this hospital as reputable. They want me in Maryland or Massachusetts. They think I can't learn what I need to learn here, and I don't want to move away. I want to prove to them that no matter where I am, I will get the education I need. I can be successful."

The more she spoke, the more I felt my heart becoming invested in her story. I could physically feel the weight she was under trying to prove herself to her parents. Mine would have been happy if I'd have just ended up as a general practitioner or even just a nurse. They'd have been proud because I finished college and did something they couldn't do. I was the golden boy in their eyes.

Sophia had all this legacy to live up to, especially with siblings who were already following that path. And with a name like Chen, I imagined her parents were probably very strict too. Call it a stereotype, but I'd heard that Asian cultures really pushed their children to excel, and for good reason. It produced highly educated and high-performing adults. I just saw the pressure it was putting on her shoulders.

"Then I'll help," I told her, speaking from my heart, not from my brain. I winced inwardly as I realized I was taking on more work at a time my ex was pushing me to back off and be there for Leah. But I couldn't very well let my student flounder due to family pressure. I pulled a card out of my desk drawer and a pen, then scrawled my personal cell phone number on it. "Here, my personal line. I think we should do more one-on-ones."

Sophia took the card from my hand and looked at it thoughtfully, then narrowed her eyes. "Won't Dr. Briggs be jealous that you're devoting more individual time to my training?" Her tongue flicked over her bottom lip, drawing my gaze away from her eyes, and I smiled at her thoughtful heart.

"I have to say, Dr. Chen, I've never had a student with such promise before. I don't think my offering you extra attention outside of our mandatory schedule will affect anything. Besides, Dr. Briggs is a professional." I looked up as my door swung open without a knock and my first instinct was to feel frustrated by the interruption.

Then I saw the bright green eyes of my baby girl and the broad grin on her face as she waltzed into the tiny space like she owned it. Her red hair had been tied up into pigtails. The designer sweater she wore was stained—evidence that Dana was still making poor choices. Buying a child a three-hundred-dollar sweater made no sense. She could've gotten the thirty-dollar knock-off and when it got stained, it would've been no big deal.

"Daddy!" Leah squeezed past the end of my desk and the door banged into the wall. My attention was focused on her as she wrapped her arms around my neck and kissed me on the cheek with sloppy lips. "I'm coming to your house again. Can we play Candy Land?"

I chuckled and hugged her back, then noticed Dana walk in with a glower on her face. She held Leah's backpack in hand, dangling it from an extended finger that had an inch-long red fingernail. It appeared she was still finding a way to make good use of all my alimony.

"You are late again, for the fourth time this month." Dana glanced at Dr. Chen as Leah stepped back. Her chubby little hand stayed on my shoulder, but she looked up at her mother and seemed intimidated or afraid. Dr. Chen looked down at her lap where she held my card with my number on it. I felt bad for her having to see this interaction.

"We had a surgery run late and we were just doing our debriefing. I should've called." I noticed how Dana wore three-inch spiky-heeled boots and jeans that looked like they were painted on. She had wasted no time diving back into the dating scene after leaving me. It was probably because she had checked out of our relationship long before the divorce was filed.

"You're right. You can't just pick and choose when to be a dad. I had plans tonight, and now I'm not even sure if they're still on." Dana dropped the backpack on the corner of my desk and huffed. She looked down at Dr. Chen and scowled, as if she'd seen that card and didn't approve. Dr. Chen had no reason to hide that from anyone, though I felt an inkling of uneasiness now, knowing Dana saw that Sophia had my personal number. It was for work purposes, but somehow, even that felt inappropriate.

"I have that fundraiser tomorrow, remember?" My chest was tight. I didn't want this to turn into a public meltdown while my intern was watching.

"Christ, Jack. It's your weekend!" She huffed and scowled at me, then crossed her arms over her chest.

"It's only for a few hours." There was no way out of this. I was required to attend the event to raise money for the hospital.

"Fine, then have her back by four Sunday. I have dinner with my parents." Dana turned and walked out the door, leaving it standing wide open, and Lean turned to me with a frown.

"I don't want to go to Nanny's house. She's so mean." Leah draped her arms around me again and rested her chin on my shoulder. Unfortunately, there was very little I could do to help her. Leah had partial custody and her mother was Leah's grandmother.

"I know, baby." I patted her back and looked up at Dr. Chen, whose face was flushed again. She really had to get over that embarrassment and low self-confidence, but I thought it was sweet that she sat there so awkwardly, fiddling with my card.

"Who's that?" Leah asked innocently.

"That," I told her, holding her at arm's length, "Is Sophia. She's a doctor I work with."

Leah cocked her head and asked, "Does she do surgery too?"

Sophia smiled, and I swore her blush deepened. "Yes, she is very good at it."

Leah walked around my desk and put her hand out like she'd seen me do a million times. It was a drawback to my profession that my little girl had to join me at work at least five times a month. I had virtually no personal time at all, and what little I had was shared with a seven-year-old.

"I'm Leah. My daddy is the best surgery guy ever." I loved my little girl's confidence.

But when Sophia reached out and took her hand and smiled, I found myself swooning a little. Sophia's eyes sparkled as she said, "I know he is. I get to learn everything he teaches me." She shook Leah's hand and then her eyes swept up to meet my gaze. I didn't know what was happening to me, but I liked it, yet at the same time, I felt like it was wrong.

I shouldn't have been looking at my intern like this, like someone I could see myself falling for. But there I was, admiring how she and my daughter talked about me like I was the most amazing man in the world, and all I could do was try to suppress a stupid grin.

When Sophia stood to leave, I asked, "Are you going to the fundraiser?" I was hopeful. For some reason, I was looking forward to it this year, and if Sophia was going, it would give me a chance to interact with her outside of work, which I told myself was strictly professional, to get an idea of her personality when she wasn't under pressure.

"Yes, I'm going." She smiled and stood by the door, then said goodbye to Leah. Then she was gone and I was left with only my anticipation of seeing her for that fundraiser. It might prove to be a very good night.

7

SOPHIA

I strolled around the ballroom at the Ritz-Carlton carrying my glass of champagne, which wasn't really champagne. Most people didn't understand that what we Americans considered champagne was just sparkling wine. I'd been to France and had the real thing before. This was nothing like it. But it helped me loosen up a little, so three glasses in, I was feeling pretty good.

"Sophia!" I heard, and I turned over my shoulder to see one of my father's old friends. A woman in her fifties by the name of Sandra Brown, a pediatric ortho with a big reputation. She was a kind woman, so I didn't mind stopping to say hello.

"Sandra," I cooed, offering the obligatory hug and cheek kiss. "It's so good to see you."

"How's your father?" she asked while my eyes scanned the crowd. I was glad that for once, Mom and Dad weren't at the function. They had jetted off to New York City for the weekend so Mom could enjoy a slice of her favorite cheesecake from her favorite little bakery. It hadn't stopped Dad from proffering a huge donation, though, which was why I was forced to attend this gig.

But my eyes were searching for Jack, not for other people I may know. From the minute I found out he was going to be here, my entire attitude about the night changed. He had given me his personal cell phone number, and while I knew he probably meant it just for work purposes, I couldn't help but get a rush of excitement. After Maylin laid it on thick about how hot he was, I couldn't think of Jack any other way now.

"He's good. They're in New York, but he sends his love." I tried not to seem too distracted, and when I didn't see Jack, I focused on Sandra's face.

Dad always came to these things, and since the time I was old enough to act respectfully, he'd been dragging me around to them too. Not just me—our whole family. He thought it was good for us to be cultured and learn how to rub elbows with the elite. Dad had made his fortune off being one of the best surgeons in the country, accepting kickbacks from pharmaceutical companies, and a lot of wise investments. I was just along for the ride.

"Oh, I'm so sad he's not here. I was hoping to catch up." Sandra gestured with her hands as she spoke, and I had to take a step backward to avoid getting swatted. I noticed a man in a black tux across the room, and when he spun around, I recognized him. Sandra went on about meeting up with my dad, but I had to stop her. My entire reason for coming just manifested.

"Sandra, if you'll excuse me," I told her, but I didn't wait for a response. I walked away, weaving through the crowd toward Jack, who held a glass identical to mine in his right hand. His dark, wavy hair wasn't tied back under a scrub cap. It was refreshing to see how handsome he was, even more so than I had noticed.

His broad shoulders fit his jacket nicely, and his slacks had a crisp crease down the front of them. He didn't notice me approaching at first, and I had the opportunity to admire his stubble and the dimple that peeked out when he smiled. I was focused on trying to make my heart stop skipping beats when I realized he was smiling at me. And it wasn't a polite "Hi, we work together" sort of smile.

"Dr. Chen," Jack said, relaxing his shoulders as his eyes scanned the length of my body. I felt a bit unnerved, like he might have been undressing me with his eyes. It wasn't an altogether uncomfortable feeling, except that he was my boss and we were supposed to be here to raise funds for our job—which prohibited the fraternization of employees.

"Please, it's Sophia," I told him. My hands felt shaky, my palms sweaty. Maylin had gotten into my head good this time. No longer was this Jack Thornton, MD, specialty surgeon who'd made waves with his career thus far. He was just a really hot guy I enjoyed looking at who just happened to have so much in common with me that I could talk to him for hours and not get bored.

"Sophia." He smiled again, and it made my body grow very warm. I felt like the tight-fitting dress I wore had suddenly turned to wool and was suffocating me with warmth.

"I'm happy to see you here. I thought you wouldn't be able to get a sitter." I sipped my drink and remembered the awkward interaction in his office between him and his ex-wife, who acted more like a spoiled child than an adult.

Jack's eyes flashed with something I couldn't really place, but my assumption was that it was frustration. I couldn't imagine dreaming about a life with someone and beginning to build something, then having that person decide they don't want to be with you anymore. His heart must have been broken pretty badly, especially given that they had a child together.

"Dana has her." His tone was gruff, but he wasn't upset with me. I could see the tension in his shoulders, though. "She'll bring Leah by when my two hours are up."

I sighed and wished I wouldn't have brought that topic up. I could tell when I watched them interacting that he and his ex weren't on very good terms. It appeared Jack wanted to keep things positive for his daughter's sake, but it didn't feel like his ex had the same intentions. She was just rude to him.

"You love your daughter very much, don't you? You're a good father. Don't let your ex-wife tell you otherwise." I knew the rigors of the profession I chose and wondered how I'd ever make it work if I had a child. I knew people did it all the time, but I didn't envy Jack the least bit.

"Thank you. You seemed to be a natural with her when she talked your ear off last night." His smile returned, and he gazed at me over the rim of his champagne flute as he sipped. He was more casual than at work, which might have been due to the strong scent of alcohol on his breath. I knew the few drinks I'd already consumed had helped me relax a bit too.

"I love kids. I'd love to have a big family someday." I glanced at a passing waiter who carried a tray with glasses, some empty, some full. Jack set his empty glass down on it as the man passed and paused for a moment as Jack plucked two full glasses off the tray. Seeing his actions, I downed the rest of my drink and set my empty glass down too.

"Walk with me," he said smoothly as he handed me a glass.

The room was full of doctors, nurses, and administrators from Twin Peaks. We had each paid a large sum to be here, or in my case, my father had. The entire night was all about making money for the hospital, but it didn't stop anyone from having a good time. We weaved through the crowd and noticed more than one of our coworkers a bit inebriated. I felt the buzz myself, which probably wasn't the best thing for my newfound fascination with my boss.

"It's not easy doing the job we do, Sophia. It takes a toll on your life at times." He walked at a respectful distance, but I found myself gravitating toward him—both physically and emotionally. I could see the longing in his eyes and wondered why I'd never noticed this softer side of him before. He was so professional on the clock, or maybe it was the drinks we'd both had.

"I think you're doing a fantastic job. Your daughter obviously loves you a lot." I sipped more champagne and realized I was not going to be able to drive myself home. I needed to order an Uber, the way things were going. And my feet hurt from being on them for so long. Every step was painful.

"Well, thank you for that, but sometimes kids don't know what's best for them. Sometimes I feel like a failure, like I should be spending more time with my daughter than I do. What if Dana's right and Leah will grow up to resent me for being too busy?" He stopped and turned to face me, and I saw the vulnerability in his expression.

We stood in a dim hallway close to the back exit of the hotel. I could still hear the din of the crowd pulling at me, reminding me that we were at a work event, but this conversation felt personal. My heart went out to him. I figured most parents felt the same way, second-guessing themselves and hoping they were doing the right things.

"You're a fantastic father, Jack, and the reason I know that is because a bad father wouldn't even stop to care whether they were making the right choices." I smiled softly at him, and he turned to stare out the window. As he did, I dipped into my clutch, dangling from my arm, and got out my phone. Then I swiped to order an Uber to take me home and slid my phone back into my purse. When he turned back toward me, I was ready to focus on only him.

"Thank you for saying that." He pursed his lips and studied my face. "I wish that Dana had even had a tiny shred of compassion like you. Things would have been so different with her." His head hung, and I felt so sad for him.

"It was a rough divorce?" I asked, stepping closer to him. We were only a few feet apart anyway, but this put me close enough to get a whiff of his cologne, and I swooned.

"Not good at all, but I'm trying to stay positive and keep my cool when I interact with her. I don't want Leah to see us fighting. She needs stability, not drama." Jack seemed to inch closer too.

The magnetic pull sucked me in like gravity. I just kept hearing Maylin's voice telling me to loosen up and flirt a little. She swore it would help me be a bit distracted so I wouldn't take the job so seriously that I freaked myself out. But Jack didn't need a flirtatious intern. I felt like what he needed was a good friend.

"I think you're doing a good job." I couldn't resist reaching out and taking his hand and squeezing it. I meant it in a friendly way, like physical touch would anchor him in the current moment and by doing so, he'd forget the past a little. But when I went to pull away, he weaved his fingers through mine and held my hand.

It sent a rush of energy through me and made my belly flutter. I swallowed hard as his gaze met mine and all the blood in my body seemed to be in my cheeks at the same time, burning and making me so flustered I almost choked on my own spit. I coughed a little and cleared my throat, then downed the rest of the champagne, which I knew would only make me more tipsy.

"Thank you for being a good friend, Sophia. I know we only just started working together, but I feel like it's going to be an amazing thing." He stepped closer, and I clenched my jaw briefly.

"You do?" I asked, watching his eyes dip to my lips.

"I do, and at the risk of being overly forward, I'd like to confess something." He didn't wait for me to respond. He just started making his confession which made me squirm with attraction. "I think you're beautiful and smart. And I've been feeling a little distracted at work by that."

His feet inched closer. My body leaned in. Was it the alcohol or was it that I really thought he was a pretty incredible man too? I wasn't sure.

"Jack, I called an Uber." It felt weird saying his name out loud like that. I'd thought of him as "Jack" all night, but not using his formal title felt like I was doing something very wrong. Shame tried to creep in, but he reached up, loosing his grip on my hand, and cupped my cheek.

"Stay. I'll take you home when I sober up." His eyes flicked back and forth on my face, searching me, and I bit my lip. The chemistry between us zinged across my skin. He was looking at me like he wanted to kiss me, but how the heck had this even happened? I wasn't making it up in my head when I sat across from him in his tiny closet of an office and I thought he was checking me out.

I wanted to protest, but I also didn't want anything to stop the train now that it had left the station. I wanted him to kiss me. I wanted Maylin to be right and for me to be able to snap out of my insecurities and use the momentum of this awkward moment to break out of my self-conscious reactions.

"I already called the Uber. They'll be here any minute." Why was I shying away, then? Why was I feeling like this was so wrong and we'd get caught and everything would blow up in my face? My father would be so upset. He'd say I brought shame on my family.

"Then I should probably do this while I have the courage, because I'm not the type of man to drink on the job and I'm pretty sure this alcohol is giving me the balls to take a chance." Jack leaned down and hovered his mouth close to mine.

I clutched the champagne flute in my hand so tightly I thought I'd snap it in half as his lips brushed mine lightly. Then he whispered, "Is this okay?"

All I could do was nod.

Jack's lips claimed mine again, this time with a ferocity that surprised me. I kissed him back too, searching his mouth with my tongue and letting him suck my lower lip into his mouth. This was going to end so badly. I could already feel it in my bones. I just couldn't help myself. After doing what everyone else told me to do my whole life, I wanted this for me.

8

JACK

When the horn honked, I knew it was Sophia's Uber. I pulled away and looked down at her kiss-swollen lips. Her eyes were starry, glistening with emotion. She was so beautiful, and I didn't need the four glasses of champagne I'd downed to know that. But I was a fool. She was very young and I was her boss. I'd crossed a line which should she decide she was uncomfortable with, it would cost me my entire career.

"I, uh... I have to go," she said, stepping backward. She held out her empty champagne flute, and I took it from her hand. "See you Monday," she said, and even through the haze of the buzz I had going, I knew I had done a very bad thing.

Sophia hurried out the doors into the darkness and climbed into the Uber driver's car. I stood there watching her, admiring her lean form and the curve of her ass in that dress until she was out of sight. I had opened myself up to a sexual harassment lawsuit and I knew it. Worse than that, I had opened a huge can of worms.

We worked together, and the hospital was very strict about their non-fraternization policy. It was in place to make sure there was no favoritism given, or so that emotions didn't interfere with the treatment of patients. Now all I would do was be distracted by her and my desire for her. That part of the alcohol's courage that I'd tapped into was a downfall. It gave me the guts to let my real desires come out, even when they stood at odds with what was right or what was ethical.

I sighed and turned back toward the ballroom. I knew when I was dressing for the event this evening that in my heart, I had unethical intentions. The more I interacted with Sophia, the fonder of her I became. I had worked with dozens of women over the years, but not a single one had piqued my interest. But Sophia Chen? She got under my skin by just being sweet and smart and backward. She was beautiful, but I couldn't see that until I saw her, and I liked what I saw when I looked at her heart.

I set her empty glass on a table, then downed mine and sat in a chair to wait for the alcohol to wear off. I watched the crowd filter in and out. A few doctors waved at me, and a few nurses said hello in passing, but most everyone just left me alone. I credited the scowl etched on my forehead. The night had gone exactly as I hoped it would, but the result in the end bit me.

If she had stayed, we would have continued to interact and I would have continued to nurse this growing infatuation. It was good that Sophia went home. We would have crossed more lines than just a harmless kiss if she had stayed here. At least, if my personal feelings toward her got what they wanted.

And how did I know that she wanted to kiss me as badly as I wanted to kiss her? I didn't. For all I knew, she kissed me out of peer pressure, thinking as her boss, I'd reprimand her or fire her for disappointing me. I'd been a manager for a while now. I knew how positions of authority tended to push people to just please their boss.

Rubbing my forehead, I closed my eyes and wished I could take it back. But the image in my mind of Sophia in that dress, smiling at me, looking up into my eyes shyly, only made me wish she were here to do it again. I liked her—a lot more than I should've.

After an hour had passed, I looked at my watch and decided I had sobered up enough to drive. Dana would bring Leah to me, but there was no point in waiting around this fundraiser alone when I could just go pick up my little girl and spend time with her. I'd made my obligatory appearance and my duty here was done. So I got in my car and drove carefully across town to Dana's house.

When I walked up to the front door, she opened it and burst outward at me, yelling something over her shoulder at Leah. She looked angry and rushed and almost ran right into my chest.

"Jack, why are you here?" Dana's question didn't come out sounding like pleasant surprise. She sounded more annoyed than anything. The glare on her face matched her tone too.

"I got done early. I thought I'd save you the trip." I stood on the sidewalk down two steps from Dana, who seemed to tower over me now with the height difference.

"Leah! Now!" she shouted, and I almost winced. I hated how she was so angry and loud at times. It made me angry with her, but I used self-control so I wasn't shouting around our daughter.

"Dana, please. Do you have to scream like that?" My head was starting to throb just thinking about the nightmare I'd created for myself at work by not keeping my thoughts and feelings to myself. And it wasn't that I'd opened up to Sophia about my personal life. I'd vented to coworkers before. It was that I was attracted to her and I liked her, and I knew there was no putting that cat back in the bag.

"Look, if you teach your kid to behave and do what she's told when she's told, I won't have to scream at her. And if you spent half the time with her that you spend at work, you'd be a real father." Dana's harsh words stung, but I clenched my jaw rather than biting back at her.

Leah appeared in the doorway and smiled. "Daddy!" She grinned and raced across the front porch, jumping into my arms. I caught her and hoisted her up into my arms. She was getting too big for this sort of affection, but I refused to make her grow up if she wasn't ready.

"Let's go home, baby. I want to do some fun stuff tonight." I didn't even say goodbye to Dana, and neither did Leah. We struck up a conversation about which board game we'd play even as Dana shouted out her reminder to have Leah back by four tomorrow.

The whole drive home, Leah told me about the exciting things happening in her school. They were taking a field trip to an art history museum. She got picked to play pickleball with a group of older kids. She was allowed to read morning announcements for her teacher, and best of all, her grade card said she had all As, which I praised her for while ensuring that she understood grades weren't everything, and she was loved for who she was, not what she did.

I wished I could tell her how excited I was to have made this weird connection with a coworker, but a seven-year-old's mind just couldn't comprehend the significance of it. Besides, I knew Dana was already dating, but even after the few years it had already been, I didn't feel right. I didn't want Leah to feel like I had moved on and forgotten her.

I also felt like if or when this blew up, it might mean my getting a lot more time with my daughter. I didn't think any reputable hospital or practice would hire me if Sophia sued for sexual harassment.

What had I done?

9

SOPHIA

I thought I had shaken it. I really did. I spent all day Sunday just focusing on self-care. I went for a long walk and did yoga. I got ice cream and soaked in a hot bath. I studied my note cards—this time without Maylin annoying me—and I hadn't thought of Jack more than a few times.

But this morning, the instant I walked into the hospital, the only thing I could think about was his lips on mine. I smelled some man's cologne in the elevator and it resembled the scent of Jack's. Then I scolded myself for thinking of him as "Jack" instead of "Dr. Thornton". I washed my face in the women's restroom and tried focusing on more things I knew I had to improve on as far as my job went, but all my hard work of stuffing my attraction to him into the darkest corner of my mind was pointless the instant he walked into the room.

Dr. Briggs and I heeded Jack's call, following him out into the hallway. We had that patient last week who had an appendectomy and we had to go through his final check before we dismissed him. Usually, the attending did stuff like this, but I was still learning and apparently, Jack decided it would be good for me to do.

We stood in the hall outside the patient's room looking over all his test results and blood work, and I was so close to Jack I could touch him. He seemed laser focused, while I kept feeling flustered and over-whelmed. He smelled good and he was so good-looking. His words oozed charm and intelligence, which only made things worse. He was hot and he was smart, and I felt like we needed to have a discussion to clear up what was going on.

"So, what do you see?" he asked me, handing me the tablet in his hands. The patient's chart was open on the screen and the results readout showed above normal numbers for his white cell count.

"The infection is abating but still present. I suggest we..." I froze, staring at the screen. My brain felt fried. I didn't know if we should send him home with the infection still lingering. After the surgery and removing more of his cecum, Jack advised a longer stay to ensure the infection was gone before he went home. A man this age would have more trouble fighting the infection, and with a comorbidity of diabetes, it made sense. "I think we..." I fumbled for words and looked up at Jack as Dr. Briggs jumped in.

He sighed hard and huffed at me. "We give another shot of antibi-otics and monitor for twenty-four more hours. That or we can send him home with a stronger broad-spectrum with instructions to have a follow-up in three days."

I winced as Jack narrowed his eyes at me and turned to my co-intern. "Good, but next time, let Dr. Chen answer. Now, Dr. Chen, what antibiotic should we put him on, and which measure do you suggest we take?"

My heart hammered and my palms were so sweaty I almost dropped the tablet. I looked back down at the screen and scrolled through the screens. It was like I forgot how to navigate the entire software. I couldn't find where it showed what antibiotic he was on right now or where it showed his other medications. I swore he was on Metformin, but where it listed it was a mystery to me in my flus-tered state.

"Just a second, I..." I let my words trail off as I swiped through the different panels in the software but still found nothing.

"Geesh," Dr. Briggs said, snatching the tablet away.

I winced as I saw Jack's scowl and I felt so foolish. This was all my fault. I had let my sister play with my head and I knew the ethical implications of that. My parents would be so ashamed of me. I was ashamed of me. I just wanted to go back to the standard of professionalism we had last week, where Jack was just my boss and I was just the skittish intern.

"Here." Dr. Briggs handed the tablet back, and it was on the screen with the patient's medications. But it was too late. I had upset Jack and he took the tablet away from me.

"Dr. Briggs, would you please go order a round of ceftriaxone and another stick tomorrow? Tell the patient he'll be released as soon as his numbers drop." Then he turned to me. "Dr. Chen, please come with me."

I followed Jack up the hallway toward the doctors' lounge with my head hanging. I felt like a puppy who had done something bad and was about to be scolded. I hated the feeling, but worse, I hated myself. I was the one who couldn't hold it together and I was making it awkward, so I was really glad when the doctors' lounge was empty and Jack shut the door behind us.

"What the hell is going on?" he hissed, and his scowl was so severe I thought he'd bite my head off. "Normally, you're socially awkward. You're never this bad." He crossed his arms over his chest and made his biceps bulge. I was sure he didn't mean to do it to provoke a reaction from me, but I couldn't help but notice.

"I'm so sorry. I'm just…" I bit my lip and looked away. "I am having a hard time focusing around you. That kiss just keeps being stuck in my head. I just…"

"Okay, wow." Jack sighed and ran a hand over his face. His hair, which was loose and wavy on Saturday night, was bound under a scrub cap again, but it didn't detract from how handsome he was. "Look, I spent the last two nights regretting that. Okay? I've been nervous you were going to bring it up. I don't want it to interfere with our work, but clearly, it will. I in no way intended to use my position as your boss to manipulate you into doing that and—"

"No, please." I almost called him Jack out loud. Doing that at an after-hours fundraiser was one thing. Doing it while on the clock was a huge no-no. "It was my fault. I'm the one who initiated physical touch by holding your hand. We just... I just... I need this internship so bad. I can't mess it up."

"And this" —his finger pointed at me, then at himself— "can't happen. We work together and it's against hospital policy. Not to mention it will only cloud our judgment for work and make it harder for us to truly function."

To me it sounded more like he was trying to convince himself that he didn't want it to happen, not that it was off limits. And that only made the monster inside me hungrier. I liked that he liked the kiss, that he was trying to fight off his own temptation. But it made no sense why I'd nuke my own job and career path over a man who was way too old for me and out of my league. My parents would never approve.

"And I have so much studying to do. I really need the one-on-one time with you without it being distracting to me. My entire future is riding on proving myself in this job and to my parents." I chewed the inside of my own cheek, now trying to convince myself it couldn't happen too. There were so many reasons.

"My job is what supports me and my daughter. If HR found out something was going on, I'd be fired. I can't risk that." Jack sucked in a deep breath and jammed his hands into his pockets and shook his head. "It's just a bad idea. We'd get involved and when things didn't go well, we'd be bickering at work. Someone would find out."

"And I need to focus on really learning. You can't teach me if you're distracted by frustrating emotions or sexually charged tension between us." I wiped my hands down the front of my scrubs nervously and wondered if Jack had been standing this close the entire time.

"And with my one-on-one time with you and the extra coaching, I barely have time for my daughter. I'd never have time for a relation-ship." Jack's eyes dropped to my lips and I licked them, feeling the tension building. I knew it wasn't just me. He was moving closer. His hands had come out of his pockets and he cracked his knuckles.

"Oh, we can do that at the same time. Your little girl is so sweet. I don't mind sharing the time with you so you get more time with her.

She could help me study." I was breathless and Jack was inching toward me.

"I just... I'm not sure if I can focus on helping you with her around, but that's a very helpful suggestion, and..." His words hung in the air as he focused on my mouth.

My heart pounded again and my God, did I want him to kiss me. I knew it was wrong, and we had just listed every single reason it couldn't happen, but here we were, about to make the same damn mistake.

"Jack, I..." I couldn't even protest because I wanted him.

"Dr. Thornton, there you are." Dr. Briggs's words halted Jack's forward momentum and he swallowed hard, his Adam's apple bobbing briefly before he turned to my co-intern. Saved by that interruption—or maybe not. Maybe I didn't feel relieved. Maybe I felt really ticked that he'd walked in just when he had.

Of course, that was better than him walking in and seeing us kissing. Yes, definitely better. This couldn't happen.

So why did I still want it to?

10

JACK

After a long day, the last thing I wanted was to disappoint Leah by telling her I had to cover an on-call shift tonight, and Dana would have thrown a fit. So, having no other choice, Leah joined me at the hospital. She sat across from me at the small dinette set in the on-call room with her workbook doing her homework as I typed my recorded patient visits into my computer to keep the transcript. She was quiet and well behaved, and we'd done this a few times before now. I had a few nurses who would step in and help watch her if I got called away.

"Daddy, what's this word?" Leah asked, pushing her notebook toward me. I glanced down at the page full of English terms and their definitions. She was supposed to match the term with its meaning by drawing a line from one to the other.

"It says, 'friend'. Do you know what that means?" I pushed the book back toward her and she grinned.

"That means Sophia. She's your friend." Leah's huge smile beamed, and I found myself smiling back at her.

"Yes, Sophia is a friend. Now finish your homework so we can watch a movie." I nodded at the book, hoping she didn't bring up my beautiful infatuation again. Sophia and I had a rough week. If she wasn't being flustered and distracted by me, I was gawking and admiring her poise and beauty.

That one little kiss had been the spark that ignited the forest fire of desire I felt in my body every time someone even said her name. I tried to focus back on my recording and transcribing the conversation, but I found myself staring at the screen, not really listening. Instead, my mind was fixated on this afternoon's interaction and how Sophia brought up our one-on-one session.

I winced and pinched the bridge of my nose. I was supposed to have met with her right now, in my office. I had been so busy trying to work out arrangements for Leah to be with me that I totally forgot I was meeting with Sophia.

Glancing at the time on my screen, I shut the laptop and stood. "Baby, I have to go to my office real quick. I'll be right back. You just do your homework, okay?"

Leah didn't even look up as she said, "Okay, Daddy." Her attention was fixed on her homework and I slipped out the door.

Before I even rounded the corner, I bumped into the person I was looking for. "Dr. Chen," I said hastily, watching the stack of index cards from her hand flutter all over the hallway.

"Oh, gosh, I'm so sorry. I wasn't watching where I was going." Sophia dropped to her knees and started scooping up the cards. I crouched alongside her and helped, feeling bad for running her over.

"I totally forgot I was helping you tonight." I felt foolish kneeling in this hallway as nurses walked past watching us, though they didn't say anything to us.

"It's okay if you don't have time. I know you're pretty busy." Sophia sounded disappointed, and I felt bad for that too.

"Not at all. I just have Leah here with me. We're in the on-call room. We can go over some things there if you don't mind a seven-year-old doing her homework."

Sophia looked up at me and smiled as I handed her the stack of cards I had collected from the floor. She added them to her stack and nodded at me. "I don't mind at all. I really appreciate your taking time to help me." We both stood, and when I stretched to my full height, I realized for the first time how much taller I was than her. Her petite frame probably only rose to my shoulder. I thought it was cute.

And the way a single dark strand of hair snuck out of her scrub cap and hung by her temple made my fingers itch to tuck it behind her ear. I was used to seeing her makeup-less face and hospital scrubs, but tonight she looked more beautiful than normal. Maybe it was the lighting, or maybe I was just paying more attention.

"Should we go, then?" she asked nervously, glancing around the hallway while I stared at her like an idiot.

"Oh, uh... Yes." I turned and walked back around the corner and dipped into the on-call room. Leah wasn't at the table with her book anymore. She was on the bed with the Xbox remote in her hand, staring up at the screen mounted on the opposite wall. Her homework looked finished, and she grinned at me when I walked in.

"Daddy, what movie can we watch?" Her eyes lit up when Sophia followed me into the room and she tossed the controller and dashed over toward us. "Sophia, you're here! Want to watch a movie with me?"

I watched Sophia's eyes trace a line from Leah's face to the workbook on the table and then back to mine. She smiled and chuckled, then said, "I have to do a bit of homework. Maybe you can help me first? Then we can watch a movie. I heard there is a new superhero show."

Leah clenched her hands into fists by her face and shook a little as she grinned. "Yes! I will help. Then we will watch a movie." She reached up and snatched Sophia's hand and pulled her toward the bed. It was cute watching them interact. I shut the door and turned to see Sophia trying her hardest to sit up on the bottom bunk. Leah was able to sit up easily, but Sophia was a few inches too tall for that.

She hunched over and started sorting her cards, and I felt sorry for her. I grabbed two chairs from the dinette set and dragged them over, then positioned them so that she and I could sit facing each other while Leah sat on the bunk.

"Oh, thank you," Sophia said, blushing. She climbed off the bed and sat in the chair, and Leah took her stack of cards with a bit of authority. I'd seen the way she took charge while interacting with friends after school sometimes. I knew it was the influence of being an only child and being surrounded by adults who were constantly telling her to do things. She had a bit of an edge, but Sophia didn't seem to mind.

"Okay, we're gonna do English now. That's what I do too. My teacher, Mrs. Kaup, calls it reading, but the book cover says *English.* That's what my mom said." Leah spoke in such a matter-of-fact way, sounding like a grownup, that I couldn't help but chuckle.

Sophia gave me a surprised but cheeky look, playing along. "Alright, Mrs. Thornton, you're my teacher tonight. I have to know all my vocabulary words. Can you read these cards?"

Leah held one up and scrunched her nose at it. "In-ci-sion," she announced proudly, and I was surprised she could sound it out. I knew the difficulty of all of the medical terms Sophia would be brushing up on were well beyond Leah's reading level or her comprehension. Hearing her use phonetics well was impressive.

"Well done," I told her. "Now you give me the card and when Sophia says the answer, I'll tell her if she's right."

Leah handed me the card and Sophia rattled off the definition. I had to help Leah sound out several of the terms when she started to get frustrated by it. Sophia cheered her on too, encouraging her, especially when Leah got to the word "resect." Leah turned the card over and read Sophia's definition— well, most of it.

"Remove part or all of an or-gan, tiss-ue, or st... Str..." She scowled. "I can't read this word."

"Structure." Sophia tousled Leah's hair. "Hey, well done. That's a very big word for a first grader. You did really good."

Leah beamed with pride and then looked up at the TV. "Daddy, did we study enough? Can we watch a superhero movie now?" Her nose scrunched up again, and I sighed.

I looked at Sophia, who was collecting her cards, and she shrugged a shoulder and gave me an understanding look. We hadn't gotten through even half of her terms, and the real work I wanted to do with her had been pushed to the back burner. We should have been going through virtual surgeries with the simulation software on my laptop.

"It's okay," Sophia said. She tapped her cards into a neat stack and stood up. "I can just get going. We can do this next week when you're not so busy. You should have time with Leah."

"Are you sure?" I asked, standing alongside her.

Leah was scrambling for the remote. I knew she knew how to navigate to the streaming app and pick a movie, so I focused on Sophia for the moment. I felt bad that I was the one who requested this opportunity to pour knowledge into her and she was being nudged to the side because of my personal life. On the other hand, my daughter was everything to me, and I couldn't just ignore my time with her. Not only would that make me a horrible parent, but Dana would flip out and I would feel guilty. I got so little time with Leah as it was.

"I'm sure. But thank you." Sophia turned and walked to the door, and I followed her. After such a tense week, I had actually wanted to speak with her about that kiss and how we could move past it and be professional. I was having a hard time, but I knew if we just spoke to each other like professionals, we could establish clear boundaries and eventually, we'd move past it.

Sophia opened the door and I turned over my shoulder and said, "I'll be right there, Leah." Then I slipped into the hallway next to my intern and leaned on the wall.

"I'm sorry, Dr. Chen."

"Please, when we're off duty, just call me Sophia." She tucked her stack of cards into her pocket and pulled her scrub cap off. Her hair, which I thought was tied into a ponytail, fell in loose waves, framing her face. She was so pretty I had to say something.

"Your hair looks nice like that. I wish I could see it more often." The compliment could have been just a passing comment between coworkers, but against the backdrop of that kiss and my strong attraction, I knew it was inappropriate.

"Uh, thanks," she said, sounding uncomfortable.

"I didn't mean… I meant… Gosh, I'm bad at this." I felt foolish again for the third time tonight. "I'm sorry. It just came out. I have a hard time keeping my mouth shut." It appeared to me that if I didn't put actual physical space between me and this woman in front of me, I was going to be the one to flub up again.

"It's okay. I understand." She chewed her bottom lip and smiled. "I should go. I don't want to end up kissing you again." The blush on her face when she said that sent a zing of arousal straight to my core. I grinned and chuckled.

"Why would that happen?" I asked her, and I probably shouldn't have. But I was curious to know what she was thinking. Honesty was the only way we'd get past this weird chemistry. We had to be honest with each other and ourselves. Pretending we weren't attracted to each other was only making us more flustered. If we could just acknowledge the attraction and admit that we had to contain it for the greater good, we could move past it.

"Well, because you're only the hottest doctor on staff and every time I'm around you, I think about doing it." Sophia's shoulder bobbed and her eyes shifted away from me, but I saw the smirk.

"Yes, well I think we both feel the same way." I sucked in a breath of relief and tried to muster the courage to have this honest conversation, but before I could, a nurse called my name.

I turned over my shoulder to see her rushing up. "Dr. Thornton, there's an emergency. Car crash victim. Internal bleeding. He's not stable. Two units of O-neg hung and he's on fluids, but we have to stop the bleed or he'll die."

My brain clicked over to autopilot and I nodded. "Get Tina. I need her to sit with my daughter." Then I looked at Sophia and said, "Want to assist? I could use your keen eye on this one."

"Of course. Let's go." Sophia took off toward the surgical unit, and I took five minutes to explain to Leah what was going on.

This wasn't how I saw my night or that conversation going, but an on-call doctor has to respond quickly. The conversation would just have to wait.

11

SOPHIA

Forty minutes into this surgery and my gloves were soaked with blood. It was the first time in surgery that I'd felt like I wasn't myself. We had gone over every organ, every inch of intestines and colon, and finally found the bleed on the back side of the man's liver. His cracked rib had perforated it and the bleeding just wouldn't stop. It was my eye that spotted it as I handled the suction and Jack maneuvered the scope.

The man was lucky to have gotten to the ER when he did. A few more minutes and he would've died of exsanguination. Lucky for him, Jack was the top-rated surgeon in the city, even for a chief resident. We got the bleeding stopped and his wound sutured, but not before I found myself getting a bit emotional. I blinked back the tears but I wasn't okay.

"Uh, nurse," Jack said, nodding at the patient. "Take over now. We're going to scrub out."

I didn't know how he did it. Jack stood over patients all day long with that scalpel in hand, cutting them open and repairing their insides. When routine surgeries were scheduled and planned ahead, bad things still happened. But I'd never assisted on an emergency surgery before. I was overwhelmed when the man's vitals crashed and we had to use the paddles to bring him back.

"Dr. Chen," Jack said, already moving toward the scrub station.

We scrubbed out, and I finally lost the battle with my tears. Jack was kind enough to say nothing to me as we washed and dried our hands and ditched the robes and gloves. I tore my scrub cap off the minute we were in the hallway moving toward his office and used it to wipe my tears. A few nurses looked at me strangely, but I was glad that it was past eleven at night. There weren't very many people around.

"Are you okay?" Jack asked, catching up with me.

My emotions weren't supposed to come out like this. I was a surgeon, not a baby. I should have been able to handle the situation and move on from it. The man was fine now. Sure, he had a long recovery ahead of him and would probably be in the hospital for weeks, but he was alive. We saved his life. Why was I so upset?

"I don't know," I told him honestly, but the tears didn't stop coming. He unlocked his office and opened the door for me, and I walked past him into the cramped space. He flicked the light on and shut the door, then instead of sitting in his chair on the far side of his desk, he sat right next to me. Three chairs in this room and he chose the one so close to mine that our knees touched.

"Hey, it's okay. Just talk to me." Jack's hand smoothed circles on my back, which I was certain wasn't professional etiquette. Any other boss under any other circumstance would just send me to the ladies' room to wash my face and get myself together. But Jack wasn't just any other boss. While we weren't exactly friends, he was somewhere across the line of professionality right now.

"He almost died." I looked up at him as I cried and sniffled, trying not to let snot run out of my nose. Crying was one thing. Ugly crying in front of my boss who was also my latest crush was not an option.

"He's okay." Jack's head nodded as he spoke. "But your reaction is perfectly normal. I had a mental breakdown and punched a hole in the wall of my boss's office when I lost my first patient." He chuckled and continued rubbing my back. "I had to pay for that

56

repair, which was almost more upsetting to me than losing the patient."

I couldn't stop crying. I swiped at my face with my scrub cap and Jack sighed. He looked around, as if searching for tissues. There was nothing in this office but three chairs, a desk, and a picture of his daughter framed on the corner of his desk.

"Here," he said, pulling his scrub cap off. "Use this." He handed it to me and I tried to smile, then I blew my nose on it. "You can keep it," he joked, and I sucked in a breath, trying to calm myself down.

"You really lost a patient?" I asked him, wanting to know the details. My lip quivered as I spoke and I stuttered a few breaths.

"Yes, I did. Elderly man had a heart attack and I was doing an angio to insert stents and he had a second one on the table. I couldn't save him." Jack looked remorseful as he said, "So don't be too hard on yourself for reacting this way. We have a really important and delicate job."

I was surprised that his hand was still on my back circling round and round. I liked the sensation. It was comforting. I met his gaze and asked, "How long did it take you to get over it?"

The sincerity in his eyes when he said, "I haven't," made my heart clench. "I take it with me into every surgery I do. That's why I stay laser focused and on top of things. I know how easily life slips through your fingers. I know how delicate the human body is."

His hand left my back and reached up to my face, curling one of my stray dark hairs around my ear. I sighed when he rested his hand on my shoulder and I looked down at the soiled scrub cap. "Thank you for listening." I felt marginally better, though I was sure I'd have bad dreams about that moment for weeks. I wondered if I was going to be the sort of person who couldn't get over operating room tensions.

When I looked back up at Jack, his eyes were full of compassion. "What sort of human would I be if I just let you sit and beat yourself up?" He opened his arms as if to offer a hug, and I didn't know what came over me, but I accepted the hug.

Nothing about this interaction was inappropriate. Not one thing about it was unethical or against the rules. But somehow, it stirred my desire to be close to him again. Only this time, it was worse. It wasn't the drive of sheer lust burning a hole through my core. It was a deep longing to feel the comfort of his arms. So when he started to loosen his grip, I clung to him, squeezing harder.

Jack held me for a few minutes, and when I pulled back slightly, I realized we had crossed the line. He was my boss, not my friend or brother or even a potential partner. I was putting myself in a very precarious position and I knew it. Seeking comfort from him in the form of physical contact would lead to no good. And after the conversation we had before surgery, I knew he was vulnerable too.

"I'm sorry, Dr. Thornton," I mumbled, trying to pull away. But he held me so I couldn't.

"Don't be sorry," he whispered, and I watched his eyes fall to my lips. "I have to admit I'm having a hard time right now." His gaze swept over my face, looking me in the eye, then dropped to my lips again.

"A hard time with what?" I asked, but I knew. I was having the same difficulty. I liked him holding me way more than I should have. And I wanted him to keep doing it. I wanted more than just to be held.

"That thing… we talked about." His tongue popped out and slicked his lip, then he sucked his lip into his mouth and bit it slightly. "I can't stop thinking about it, about you."

My mind was racing, and my heart was beating so fast I felt breathless. I'd gone from self-pity to desire in three seconds flat. Here was the most gorgeous man I'd ever met staring me in the eye, basically telling me he wanted to kiss me—again. But he was off limits. I shouldn't be doing it. I should have been pushing him away, doing the right thing. Following hospital policy. I should have been thinking about my parents and what they'd think, or my career and how this would turn out.

But for the life of me, as I began being sucked into his gravity, the only thing I could think of was how his lips felt on mine at that fundraiser.

"Then I think maybe you should stop thinking," I told him, and what I meant was, stop thinking about me. But what happened was the polar opposite.

Jack leaned forward and pressed his lips against mine, and I let my eyes shut as I parted my lips and let my tongue dance with his.

I felt his hands slide up my body, gently caressing my back before sliding down to cup my ass, pulling me into his lap. In a flash, I found myself straddling him on his chair, legs around his waist. The kiss deepened, and all coherent thought fled. All I could think about was how soft his lips were, how the stubble around his jawline sent shivers down my spine, how he tasted like peppermint and heat—and Jack.

It was addictive, and I wanted more. I needed more. My hands reached down to the drawstring on his scrubs, fumbling with it until his pants were undone and I could feel him straining against his boxers. He was hard for me, and it thrilled me to no end.

"Do you want this?" he asked, voice husky with need as he pulled away momentarily.

"God, yes, I want you, Jack. Please," I breathed out, and in the back of my mind, I knew we were crossing a line, but for once, I didn't care.

The kiss was so heated, both of us were panting. Jack tore my scrub top off over my head, then undid my bra as I reached into his pants and stroked him. He grunted into my mouth as I touched a particularly sensitive spot on his swollen dick, then he kneaded my breasts.

His face broke into a searing grin, one I'd never seen before, and even though I had been on the receiving end of many a smile from him, this one was different. This one was for me, for us. It was full of heat, and want, and need. Needs that mirrored my own and scared me more than I cared to admit.

He leaned in slowly, so I could back away if I wanted to. But I didn't want to. I couldn't move even if my life depended on it. All I could do was watch as his lips got closer and closer until they brushed over my chest, licking and sucking a nipple into his mouth. I hissed in pleasure and arched my back and watched as his hand reached out to click the lock on his door.

"My God, woman, you drive me insane. I've wanted to do this for days." Jack sucked a nipple into his mouth again and swirled his

59

tongue around it, and I lost my ability to think straight. My core ached to be filled.

"God, I want you so fucking bad," I moaned, then sniffled. The last traces of my sadness were actively being washed away by my growing urge for climax.

His hands were everywhere, all over me, squeezing and rubbing. And all I could do was let him molest me as I gripped his dick hard and touched my clit through my scrubs. My pussy was soaked, making my panties and scrub pants wet. And I was so aroused I'd come in like two seconds if he just took his pants off and put it in me.

"Jack, please," I whimpered, and he seemed to know what I needed.

Jack stood and tugged my pants down, then his own, before sitting back down. There was no space in this tiny room, so when I straddled him, with my scrubs and panties still dangling from one leg, my knees hit the other chair and the wall. But sliding down around his girth, which he held up for me, was exquisite. Better than I hoped for.

"Oh, shit," I groaned, feeling him sink until his cock hit my back wall. I wasn't even ready for it when he started thrusting.

"God, you feel so good. So warm and wet and tight." Jack groaned, slamming into me again and again. It was so good, the way he filled me up and pushed against my G-spot so perfectly.

"Yes, more, please," I moaned, rocking my hips in time with his thrusts. "Harder!"

He obliged without a word, one hand gripping my ass and guiding my hips as he thrust into me harder, faster. The other was around my neck, angling my face so our lips could meet in a frantic kiss. His mouth was hot and wet and demanding like his thrusts, and I loved it. I loved every second of his tongue dueling with mine while he took me to the brink of orgasm.

I couldn't believe this was happening. I had been crushing on him for weeks and he was now inside me, pounding away at my core. I lost myself, letting his thumb brush my clit and rub, and my pussy clenched around him. The orgasm came spilling over me like a waterfall, washing down and sucking me under the flow. I gasped and moaned, and his lips swallowed my cry until I felt warmth, and he pushed me backward.

His dick sprang up, dumping the white, stringy stands of cum onto his shirt and stomach, and I felt it drain from me too. He had tried to pull out but hadn't timed it right, and I felt totally stupid for not insisting on a condom.

"Oh, God, you're incredible," he breathed, then gripped his dick to slow the spurting body fluid. I slid off him, looking around for the discarded scrub cap I had blown my nose into. It lay on the floor next to my shirt.

I picked it up and wiped myself clean, noticing he had, in fact, gotten some inside me. I turned my back, hoping he hadn't seen my look of shock or fear. And then he stood and pulled his scrub top off. He tossed it to the floor and pulled up his pants, then gripped my elbows from behind and kissed the back of my head.

"I'm sorry. I didn't mean to get that in you."

"Uh, it's okay... I'm sure this isn't my fertile time. And you got most of it on your shirt," I told him, glancing over my shoulder to see his plain white T-shirt was moist on the belly. I was hiding how freaked out I was, and I hoped it was working.

"Do you think we should talk about this?" he asked, and I knew we should, but all I could do was lean back against his chest and sigh.

"Later," I told him. "I think Leah's probably waiting for you." I bent and picked up my clothing, then walked behind his chairs and stood where he could leave the room without anyone in the hallway seeing me. "Go," I told him, faking a smile.

Jack nodded and snatched his scrub shirt off the floor and darted out the door, calling, "Lock up when you leave," over his shoulder.

Wow, so I had sex with my boss and now I was standing in his office naked. It couldn't get more compromising than this.

12

JACK

I pushed Leah harder on the swing and her body launched higher into the air. Her giggles and squeals were music to my ears. I loved days off when it was nice weather and we could go to the park. It was Dana's weekend, but I caught her in a good mood—or maybe she just wanted to go out instead of having Leah today. I lucked into being able to bring my little girl out for a playdate, and I was soaking up every second of enjoyment.

"Higher!" she ordered, and I obliged. I lined up behind her, and when the swing's downward arc was complete, I ran forward, pushing on her back until she was high in the air and I could run under her to the front of the swing.

Leah giggled and laughed, kicking her feet, and I leaned down on my knees to catch my breath. We'd been all over this park today, the slides, the teeter totters, the merry go round, and even skipping rocks on the stream. Knowing our time was coming to an end and Dana would expect her home soon, I made it a point to hit the swings, Leah's favorite.

"Higher!" she squealed again, but I was done. I was exhausted from hours of playing and romping and I needed a break.

"Daddy's too tired, baby. And we have to go home soon." I straightened and noticed Leah immediately scowling. It wasn't like her to be in a sullen mood, and I felt bad that the idea of going home had upset her. But I didn't have a choice. I wasn't just being the "no-fun" parent. I wasn't even supposed to have her with me today. Dana asked me to have her home by five, and I had to listen, or little jaunts like this on special days would never happen.

I had finally gotten some time off after a grueling week of surgeries and emergencies at work, and I hoped my asking for more time with Leah was helping Dana see that I really did want to be a good father.

"I don't want to go home," Leah whined, and she dragged her feet when the swing was at its lowest point. She kicked up mulch in both directions as the swing slowly came to a lower arc then stopped. Then she sat there gripping the chains and staring at me with doe eyes. "Can't we just go to your house?"

My heart squeezed at the question. I hated that "going home" and "going to my house" were two different things. I wanted Leah to know my house was her home too, but the minute I said we had to go home, she knew it meant back to her mother's.

"I'm sorry, baby. Mommy wants you to be home for dinner at five, and it's already after four. If we don't hurry, you'll be late, and she might not like that." In the back of my mind, I was happy she wanted to be with me more, but I didn't like the insinuation that she didn't like being at home. "What's wrong with Mommy's house?" I walked over to her and crouched in front of her as she sat on the swing, and she kicked more mulch at me and it fell near my knees. Her long face troubled me.

"She's not you. I like you." Leah hung her head, but her hands still gripped the chain tightly. To see her go from being so happy to so upset with only one phrase was concerning.

"I know you like me. I like you too. In fact, I love you and I want you to be happy. But we have to follow the rules." I reached out and wrapped my hand around hers on the chain. "Why don't you like Mommy's house?"

Never in a million years did I ever think Dana would harm Leah.

63

Other than shouting at her, the woman had no motivation to even be a parent. I doubted she even had energy to get up and be physically abusive. She spent most of her time online shopping and blowing through her alimony check.

"She brings her friends over and they're mean. And I have to stay in my room and color. And one time, I colored on the wall and Mommy yelled at me." Leah's honesty was refreshing. I knew kids could lie and be little stinkers about things, but I had never worried about that with Leah. She had always been truthful to me.

"Mommy's friends?" I asked her, wondering who Dana was permitting to be around my daughter in my absence. We both had lives and that meant we had our own circles of friends. But if she was bringing harmful or dangerous people into the home, I'd have to see about stopping that.

"The mans she's dating." Leah's lip pouted out.

"You mean men?" I said, and she scowled at me.

"Sarah told me that dating is when your mom brings a man home and they eat dinner." Leah's best friend had two older sisters of dating age and after being caught trying to kiss a young boy under the bleachers at recess, that same friend had been given a detention. I wished Dana would have stepped in and not let Leah be exposed to that sort of thing, but clearly, she was too busy moving on with her life.

"Honey, why do you think those men are mean?" I asked her, prying a little. I didn't think for a second that Dana would harbor a child abuser, but I couldn't be too careful. Still, I didn't want Leah to repeat any information I said back to her mother without Dana having context for it.

"Because they tell Mommy I'm too loud and then she makes me go to bed early." She wrestled her hand away from mine and crossed her arms over her chest. "I don't like them. Can I go to your house?"

My heart broke. My little girl wasn't happy with life the way it was and I felt like it was my fault. If only I'd been able to hold things together better, Dana wouldn't have left and my family would be whole. But hindsight is twenty-twenty, and no amount of remorse or regret would go back and change the past.

I stood and held my hand out to Leah, who took it and stood with me. She walked with me with her head drooping, and we headed toward the car.

"I'm sorry, baby, but you have to wait until next weekend. You can't come to my house today. Alright?" I didn't think anything from Dana's house sounded dangerous, though I was disappointed that she didn't stand up for her own child, instead shutting her away in the bedroom to keep her "boyfriends" happy. I was wise enough to know a child sees things differently too, but I planned to be more observant just in case.

"I just wish I could be with you." Leah kicked a rock, and I decided to change the subject. Hearing about how Dana was moving on and dating was bittersweet. I never harbored any hope that we'd get back together—I was done with her after the way she handled things during the divorce. But I had mixed emotions about moving on.

Part of me felt like by adding a new woman to the situation, I was betraying my vows, though those vows had been dissolved in a court of law. But I also didn't want to do to Leah what Dana was doing. I might really hit it off with someone, but if Leah didn't like them, it was pointless. Dating would be twice as hard.

"What do you think about my friend?" I asked her thoughtfully. Leah had spent enough time with Sophia now that I figured she was able to form an opinion of her own.

This week had been so busy rushing from one surgery to another, then catching Leah's gymnastics meets on Tuesday and Thursday, I only had time for one after-work session with Sophia, and Leah had to be there again. It devolved into a game of Go Fish and a lot of laughter. Sophia and I still hadn't had that talk, but while she was on my mind, I figured I'd get my daughter's thoughts.

"Sophia?" she asked, and her eyebrows went up.

"Yeah, what do you think of her?"

I didn't have to ask her twice. Leah seemed excited to talk about Sophia. "I really like her. She says I'm a good reader, and she likes to play games. I want to watch the superhero movie with her. Last time, I fell asleep and I was waiting for you." Leah dove off into a rambling bunny trail of thoughts about Sophia, and my heart felt warm and full that my child—who seemed to very strongly dislike her mother's new paramours—enjoyed the prospect of having Sophia around more.

The conversation continued all the way across town, though I asked her to not talk about Sophia around her mother, which she promised to do. I didn't need Dana having any other reason to lecture or nag me. I didn't even know what the heck was happening between me and Sophia, and I wondered if I was setting my daughter up for heartbreak now.

The thing between me and my intern really shouldn't be happening at all, but I'd lost any semblance of self-control around her. Maybe that was why I had snatched up any patient I could to keep myself so busy this week. I couldn't face the fact that I really liked her and wanted to see where this went, because I knew it was against hospital policy. And I couldn't bring myself to tell her it had to stop now—because I didn't want it to stop.

I wanted Sophia Chen more than I had ever wanted any other woman, and that spelled disaster just waiting to happen.

13

SOPHIA

When I learned Maylin wouldn't be at family dinner tonight, I honestly breathed a sigh of relief. I didn't need her pressuring me into talking about my "hot boss" and goading me into revealing details. I was able to be as tight-lipped as an air lock on a submarine when it came to keeping other people's secrets for them—no one should ever share someone else's secrets. But when it came to my personal life, especially with my sister, who was my closest friend, I had a tendency to over share.

I carried my traditional pork and cabbage jiaozi, dumplings that were full of delicious savory meat and vegetables. I knew Mom was making her sweet and sour chicken, and the boys loved the jiaozi. I just wanted the dinner to be peaceable with no lectures. Dad loved when Mom cooked his favorites, so I figured bringing one with me could only improve his mood. After the last few weeks, I needed more points on my scoreboard.

"Oh, Soph, come in," Mom said, gesturing at me.

I walked in through the back door, having parked around back on purpose so I didn't have to enter through the living room and face Dad alone right off the bat. He'd sent me a few text messages this week indicating he'd like to discuss my internship, and I wanted to avoid that discussion for as long as possible.

"I brought jiaozi. I hope it's as good as yours." Smiling, I hoisted the casserole dish into the air and nodded at her, and she cocked her head.

"Oh, that's so good of you—Wait." Her eyes narrowed at me. "You didn't buy them from that shop on Third Street, did you?" She reached for a hand towel and wiped her hands as I opened my arms for a hug after setting the dish on the counter.

"What? And waste all that training you gave me in this kitchen? Never!" I grinned at her as I backed away, and she let her hands slide down my arms until our hands were clasped together.

"It's a sweet gesture," she said. "Thank you."

"Of course… Need help setting the table?" I asked before turning to look, but I immediately noticed the table was set, minus one setting where Maylin always sat.

"No, the boys did it already, and in fact, we're ready to eat now." Mom turned over her shoulder and called, "Food is ready, Àirén!"

I smiled at the way my parents were still so in love, calling each other lover rather than by their name. Then I made my way to the table, parking my purse on the counter and picking up my dish. I removed the lid and placed it under the dish as I sat it on the table. Steam rose from the dumplings and made my mouth water, and soon, my dish was joined by Mom's chicken, a plate of egg rolls Andrew had brought, and the smiling faces of my family who sat and started serving themselves food.

I put a dumpling and an egg roll on my plate, and Thomas dished me a helping of the chicken. Everything looked and smelled so good, we all dug in and started eating without much conversation. My stomach grumbled for more until I had several bites down, and I knew I would want to eat more. I didn't know what had come over me, but I was ravenously hungry.

"So, Baba, Mama." Thomas smiled and sighed happily. Mom and Dad continued eating but paid more attention to him as he continued. "Remember that I told you I'd met someone?" Thomas had been dating a woman from his practice for a few months now, maybe more than six. I'd lost track. He had never brought her home to meet our parents, though he did live more than a ninety-minute drive north of the city, and he worked farther north than that. If she lived north of the practice, it could have been a three-hour drive for her just to come.

"Yes, I remember," Mom said, pausing slightly. She raised her eyebrows and put her fork down on her plate. Dad merely grunted and kept feeding himself. He was so no-nonsense and never got excited about anything unless it was something that personally affected him or interested him.

"Well, her name is Elaine Hooper." He had such a dumb grin on his face it wasn't hard to figure out what he was about to say. I found myself joining in his happiness as he blurted out, "I'm going to marry her. I asked her if she would be my wife and help me build my practice, and she said yes."

Dad's head shot up, and he picked up his napkin and wiped his face, and when he lowered his hand, he had a big smile that reached his eyes. The gray in his beard had been doused in sweet and sour sauce, giving it a red tint, but he didn't seem to care.

"Thomas, that's so good." Dad stood and reached out his hand in a very formal show of happiness, too formal. I wondered how he ever survived his family with no hugs or kisses on the cheek. Thomas shook his hand and then turned to Mom, who stood and flung her arms around him.

"Oh, my little Tommy has grown up! Àirén, our boy is all grown up!" Mom's statement made my brother blush, and she held him by the cheeks and her eyes misted over. "When can we meet her? Did you pick a date yet?"

I settled into my seat, listening, and I put more food on my plate to satisfy my growing urge to binge on dumplings and engorge my stomach. I was happy. The focus of this dinner would be on Thomas and his announcement, which meant I could relax and not stress about whether my father brought up the internship. I didn't figure he'd ruin the mood of the evening by bringing up something he knew was a sour topic.

I listened to Thomas tell us all about how amazing Elaine was. She came from a mixed-culture family too, though her mother was French and her father American. The mixture of French and Chinese customs would be hard to pull off for the wedding, especially since my father would be a stickler about ensuring his traditional values were observed and who knew what Elaine's family was like. Most notably, there would be the topic of Elaine's dress, which would likely be white and not the preferred red Dad would expect.

It was humorous hearing how Thomas had to backpedal trying to assuage Dad's insistence at every turn, though I did feel sorry for him. Lately, it had been me who was under the gun and all that micro-managing had turned on my brother for now. But hearing how Elaine and Thomas met, how they wanted to honor all three cultures, and how in spite of the differences, they both wanted to have a family and teach their children all the beautiful things about both cultures made me happy.

I was ready to volunteer to help clean the table when a lull in the conversation had Dad turn his attention on me.

"I have some good news myself," he said, and though his face wasn't the broad smile it had been when Thomas told us he was engaged, I could see Dad was happy. I remained at the table to hear whatever it was that made him feel happy, and he looked straight at me. "The internship with Dr. Manning at Johns Hopkins is solidified. He will offer you the full five-year surgical residency. You can start September first, which will give us time to get you moved and situated in Baltimore."

Dad looked at Mom, whose smile was filled with apprehension. She seemed to understand I wasn't going to take this easily, but she still looked hopeful that I'd agree to it. I knew how much she wanted to keep peace between me and Dad, and while she would always side with him and probably agreed his way was best, she still understood my heart.

"Mama has found four different apartments that are within our price range. We'll set up the lease and utilities, and everything is paid for except your food budget. You won't have to worry about a thing. We just have to decide which apartment." Dad dabbed his beard and rested his napkin on his thigh under the table and waited as if I were going to thank him.

My throat felt like I got a bit of food stuck in it, so I picked up my glass of water and had a big gulp, but the lump never moved from where it was lodged in my throat. Dad had gone behind my back to line things up for me and it frustrated me. I wasn't a child anymore. At twenty-eight, I should be respected as an adult. I lived on my own, and sure, they paid my rent, but I could've paid for it myself. I'd have to cut my cable and internet, go with one of those low-cost prepaid phones, ditch the car in favor of public transport, and probably shop at a discount store instead of my normal grocery, but I could do it.

"Baba, that's so sweet of you," I started, but I just couldn't do it. I had a really great thing going at Twin Peaks. I knew Manning would never give me the one-on-one training Jack was giving me, and that was outside of the fact that there was something brewing with Jack. I needed to be here, to keep my roots, to stay close to family, and to figure out what the heck was even going on in my love life. I was addicted to Dr. Thornton.

"So Mother will help you pack your things. It's not even the first of August, so you have a full month to get things ready." He nodded as if I were just going to sit here and accept his words as directives. I should have just kept talking when I told him it was sweet, but while I did think it was sweet that he was trying, I had no intention of letting him push me around.

"Baba, I like Twin Peaks." I nervously wiped my mouth, now no longer hungry at all. Then I draped the napkin over my plate and placed my silverware on top of it.

"Twin Peaks is beneath you, Sophia. This is an opportunity to expand your potential." He shook his head, and I could see the frustration creeping into his face, around his eyes, as creases formed there. "You will enjoy this. You'll see."

"No, Baba." I stood and huffed. "I'm not going to Maryland. I want to learn from Dr. Thornton." I surprised myself by remembering to call him by his title, not by his given name. Dad wasn't at all happy about it, though. He looked up at me in frustration as it dawned on him that I wasn't going to do what he wanted. The happy and light mood that had hosted our dinner thus far had dissolved and was replaced by tension in the air.

"Sit down, Sophia. We aren't discussing this. You will have your things packed and ready by September first."

The way he spoke to me as if I were a child enraged me. "No, Baba, I won't. I'm not moving. I am going to continue my internship at Twin Peaks." I picked up my plate as tears filled my eyes, and I wished my mother would have stepped up and said something. But she sat silently with her head down in submission the way he taught her to respect him. "I'm going to clean the table now. Finish what you want to eat."

Taking my plate and glass, I walked away from the dining table into the kitchen, just out of earshot, and finally, I let my tears flow. Standing over the sink, I scraped the food off my plate into the disposal and rinsed my dishes, then loaded them into the dishwasher. And it wasn't Mom who came after me.

Andrew appeared around the corner, where no one from the dining room could see us, and set his dishes down. "Hey, come here," he said, pulling me into his arms. The embrace was comforting, but I knew he would only side with Dad, if for no other reason than not incurring my parents' wrath onto himself. Any of us children would have done the same.

"I'm not going, Drew. I want to stay here. I don't want to move away." My tears were finally abating, but my resolve hadn't waned.

"I know you don't like the idea, Soph, but if you don't do what he says, he'll cut you off. Would it really be so bad to travel a little and see more of the country? It's just five years. Then you can take whatever job you want." Andrew brushed a tear off my cheek, and I shook my head.

"Let him cut me off then. I know I can support myself. I don't need all of this," I told him, waving my hand around to indicate the wealth of my parents. I had never struggled or lacked for anything in my life, but I wasn't afraid to. "I do need to be able to choose my own path, though."

Andrew nodded, but I could see he thought I was making a mistake. "I love you, Sis," he said, then he pecked me on the cheek and walked away as I stood there fuming.

I refused to be controlled by money. I wasn't going to move to Maryland to take that job. I wanted to live in Denver. I wanted to work for Jack.

14

JACK

I walked into the room, coffee in hand, and found Chen and Briggs already waiting. They were reviewing the charts for our bowel resection case, a bad biopsy from the week before that had led us here. Normally, Sophia would be hunched over her notes, nervously chewing on her lip, but today... She was different. Confident. Composed. Almost unnervingly so.

"Morning, doctors," I said, setting down my cup. "Let's hear it. What's the game plan for the resection?"

Sophia spoke up before I had the chance to make eye contact with anyone. "Well, considering the tumor's location in the sigmoid colon, we'll need to perform a segmental resection with primary anastomosis, leaving enough of the healthy bowel to maintain function. I've already flagged potential complications—perforation, anastomotic leak, post-op ileus—and we'll need to closely monitor for ischemia post-surgery."

I raised an eyebrow. "Good catch on the complications, Dr. Chen. And what about the margins?"

She didn't even blink. "We'll aim for at least five centimeters clear on either side of the tumor to reduce the chance of recurrence. I've prepped the patient file for the OR and made sure blood products are on standby, in case we hit any unexpected bleeding."

I glanced over at Dr. Briggs, who was flipping through the chart with a furrowed brow, clearly trying to keep up. "Dr. Briggs, thoughts?"

He cleared his throat, a bit slower to respond than usual. "Uh, right. Well, I mean, what she said. Plus, we should, uh, consider the patient's age and comorbidities. Might complicate recovery, right?" It was odd to see him as the one squirming and uncomfortable.

"Right." I nodded, waiting for more. "And?"

He fumbled for a moment. "And... we need to ensure adequate pain management, post-op fluids, and... you know, the standard stuff."

Sophia shot him a brief glance, not smug, but certainly more in control than I'd ever seen her. It was enough to make him tighten his grip on the file. I wondered what had gotten into her. In the past ten days, she'd been coming out of her shell more and more, and I wondered if it was the one-on-one coaching or something more.

"Well, it sounds like you've both got the basics down," I said, not bothering to hide the amusement in my voice. "Dr. Chen, anything you'd add?"

She didn't hesitate. "I've already discussed the case with anesthesiology and flagged the patient's mild COPD. They're ready to modify the ventilation plan accordingly."

Dr. Briggs shifted, clearly annoyed. "Right, of course. I mean, I was gonna mention that."

I looked at him, then back at Sophia, who, for once, wasn't second-guessing herself. "Good work, both of you. Looks like the roles are reversing a bit today, huh, Dr. Briggs?"

He forced a smile, but there was a tinge of frustration behind it. "Yeah, seems like it. Dr. Chen's on fire this morning."

Sophia smiled politely but kept her eyes on the patient's chart, pretending not to notice his irritation.

"Alright," I said, standing up and grabbing my coffee. "Let's get this patient through surgery without any surprises. You're both scrubbing in. Dr. Chen, you can lead the resection prep."

Dr. Briggs's expression didn't change, but I could almost hear the gears grinding in his head.

Sophia nodded, calm as ever. "I'm ready, Dr. Thornton."

And for the first time, I didn't doubt her.

I let Dr. Briggs head out while Sophia and I lingered for a moment in the doctors' lounge. She stacked her notebook on her tablet and put her pen into her pocket and then hugged her things to her chest and started for the door, but I couldn't put my finger on what I found so uncomfortable with this shift in her demeanor.

"Dr. Chen, can we speak?" I turned over my shoulder in time to see her pause by the door and turn back to me.

"Of course," she said politely and hovered there. I glanced around the room and ensured we were alone and gestured with my head for her to come back.

Sophia walked over to me and stood over me, and I tried to keep myself composed. For the most part, I had been able to handle myself and push away my desire for her. At times, she was distracting in a good way, helping me stay not so serious that I took the job too personally, but not distracting enough to cause us issues. But after that sex in my office, she had changed. I didn't dislike it, but it was noticeable now.

"What's going on?" I asked, and she blinked rapidly.

"What do you mean?" Sophia looked around, and I noticed the way her bottom lip drew into her mouth between her teeth. My eyes fell there, and I had to fight the urge to stay fixed on her mouth. I wanted her again so badly I could taste it, but she was too obvious. Her entire demeanor had shifted, and even Dr. Briggs was noticing.

"I mean, quiet, backward Sophia vanished and this." I swept my hand up and down, gesturing from her head to her feet.

"I'm sorry, I just feel more confident, I guess." Her smile was brilliant, and I loved seeing this side of her. But she suddenly got a little flustered and her cheeks tinged pink.

I stood and sighed. "Because we had sex?" I asked, raising my eyebrows. I knew that was the case. She felt safer with me now, which meant she felt more confident in general, and that was contributing to her superior performance. While all of that was a good thing, the foundation of it wasn't. If that foundation crumbled—which it would the instant anyone found out and told the board we had sex—her confidence would plummet again.

"No, well... No." She shook her head, and it drooped.

"Sophia, it can't happen." I was tearing my own heart out by saying it, but it was the truth. We could not entertain the idea of a relationship or even a fling. Even the positive changes it could have between us were bad. They were affecting her performance at work and at times, they were distracting to me.

"I know," she said sadly, and she nodded her head at me. "I'm sorry." I hated that she was a wilting flower, retreating inward into her mind where in her own eyes, she wasn't capable. I wished that I could make it different for her, somehow speak life into her in a way that was ethical and professional and gave her the same confidence boost— without breaking hospital policy.

"Look, I have some free time tonight. You and I should do some one-on-one. How does that sound? I'll order pizza." I intended this time to keep it fully professional and make sure we focused on education. I had a simulator on my laptop. I'd been dying to have her try it out.

"Yes, I have time," she said, but the zest was gone from her tone. "I better go do pre-op." Sophia threw a thumb over her shoulder and backed away, and I felt sorry for taking the wind out of her sails, but it was for the best.

The farther we got from the topic of our having sex, the better. The more space we put between ourselves, the more clearly we'd see that it would never work. Because of our age difference, because of my little girl and the custody issue, because of our job, and most importantly, because if I didn't get her out of my head, I was going to make a mistake that might really hurt someone on my surgical table.

15

SOPHIA

I had to admit the simulation software Jack had me working with was pretty cool. I had done an appendectomy, a cholecystectomy, a trauma surgery, and even a gastric bypass. The system had every surgery imaginable broken down into categories for everything from orthopedic, to internal medicine, to neurological and cardiac. I was fascinated with it even if I had to use a mouse for everything and the extension remotes that paired with it weren't available. Jack said they were too expensive.

"What's that?" Leah asked me, leaning on the coffee table where Jack's laptop sat. She had been "helping" me with my practice while Jack cooked dinner for us, and now that dinner was over and he was cleaning up, she was here at my side again, distracting me.

"Uh, that's a lung," I told her, trying to focus. Jack walked in with a towel in his hands, drying them, and I could hear his scowl as he spoke to her without even having to see his face.

"Leah, I asked you to leave Dr. Chen alone. She needs to do her studying." His shift from calling me Sophia back to calling me by my title and surname felt like a slap in the face, but after our conversation this afternoon, I knew why he was doing it.

What happened between us should never have happened and we never took time to talk about it. Maybe we should have, but that night, I knew he had left his daughter in the on-call room with a nurse who had a job to do. We didn't have time right then. Then we got bombarded by a very busy week and an even busier weekend last weekend. I had plans on Saturday and my family thing on Sunday while Jack was on call all weekend.

Now, Wednesday night, and an odd night for Jack to have his daughter, we'd finally squeezed in time to do more intensive studying together, but having that conversation in front of his seven-year-old wouldn't work. Not to mention the fact that the damage was done. I could tell he was affected by the sex too, whether he cared to admit it or not. He was nicer to me, harder on Dr. Briggs, and then there were the times he just sat and checked me out so obviously.

"But she's playing a game I like to watch," Leah said innocently. "It's my favorite."

"Your favorite, huh?" Jack asked her, flipping the towel so it hung over his shoulder. Then he picked her up and tickled her. "When do you play this game?" he asked as she giggled and squirmed. Then he dropped her on the couch next to me and she sighed.

"I play at Mommy's house all the time." Leah crossed her arms over her chest confidently, and my God, I wished I had half the confidence of this child who was clearly lying.

"Now, baby, what have I told you about lying?" Jack lowered himself onto the couch beside her, and I sat back and watched the interaction. He was such a good father, not scolding and harsh like mine. His gentle correction helped coax the lie right out of her.

"I know, Daddy. I'm sorry. I just want to watch." Leah climbed onto his lap, and I smiled at the sweet interaction.

"Well, how about we read you a bedtime story instead?" I offered, glancing at the bookshelf across the room. Jack had a big collection of books, some novels, some textbooks. But there was a shelf dedicated to children's books, and Leah's eyes lit up as I said that.

"Yeah?" she said, looking at her father.

"I like that idea," he told her, and she scrambled off his lap and ran across the room. "We don't have to do this. You should be studying. Let me take her into her room and I'll read to her."

"Nonsense. I love kids. I told you that. Besides, she clearly likes me, and it's good for her to have positive role models." I waved off Jack's concern knowing I could come back and use this software any time.

Leah chose the book, *The Hungry Caterpillar*, and this time climbed onto my lap. I noticed Jack feign jealousy, but he was joking. He scooted closer to me as I opened the hard cover and started reading. Leah got so into it that she was making funny voices and reciting things the insects were saying, and I realized she had the book memorized. We moved on to another book, then another, and when she asked for a fourth, Jack drew the line.

"Bedtime, little miss." He took the books from her and set them on the coffee table, and she pouted.

"But just one more," she whined, and he was firm.

"Go put on your pajamas and brush your teeth. I'll come tuck you in." He chased her off, but before she ran out of the room, she gave me a big hug.

"See you later, Sophia," she said sadly and then ran away.

Jack chuckled. "Oh, the drama," he whined in even more dramatic tones and said, "I'll be right back.

Without skipping a beat, I dived back into the simulation. The technology was incredible. I found myself so engrossed in it that I hardly noticed that he came back into the room. Then he left again, and I heard the dishes clattering as he finished cleaning up from supper. When I finished two more quick surgery simulations, my eyes were tired. I didn't want to just leave without saying goodbye, so I decided to tidy up while waiting for Jack to come back.

I closed his laptop and turned the Bluetooth mouse off. Then I picked up the stack of books and walked over to the bookshelf to replace them, quickly finding Jack had alphabetized the whole lot. It made me grin at how organized and meticulous he was. Then my eyes scanned the towering shelf loaded with so many good titles. He had psychology books, surgical books, smutty romance novels, and one with the title, "*Addicted to Cheating*." I started to get the idea that maybe his divorce really was as unhappy as he claimed.

"Lots of good ones," Jack said, almost startling me. "You can borrow anything you like." I never heard him come back into the room, let alone walk up behind me.

"These are really great, Jack. I don't know how I'd even have time to read them all." I grinned at the odd collection and tried to just soak in the titles. He really did have similar interests and tastes as me.

"Ah, you'd be surprised. A few pages a day equates to a whole book in a few months." He reached up and pulled one off the shelf called *Abnormal Psychology*. It had a picture of a woman holding her head on the cover and just the title appealed to me. "I loved this one when I took my psych classes. So interesting how the brain works."

"But you didn't become a neurologist?" I was joking, but Jack took it more seriously.

"Not even on the cards. I was more fascinated by the internal organs and how they cooperate to make the body function." He slid the book back into its spot on the shelf and pulled another one down. "*The Basics of Saving a Life*." He tapped the cover and said, "This one is a good one. You should read it."

I scrunched my nose and took it from his hand. "It's a military book?" I asked, not understanding why he'd even have this one.

"Yes. I enlisted for a single tour, twenty-four months. After reading this in basic training, I knew I wanted to be a surgeon. Back then, it would have been a field surgeon, but they aren't given the same title or licensing as someone who went to college and graduated from med school. I left the army when my time was up and went back to school."

I looked up from the cover of the book as I heard the nostalgic tone in his voice. "Which is why you're only just chief resident at what, forty?" My honest stab at his age made him wince and press his hand to his chest as if I had mortally wounded him.

"I look that old?" he asked, chuckling, but before I could answer and feel stupid, he continued. "I'm thirty-eight, and yes. That's part of the reason I got a late start. When you don't start your bachelor's until you're twenty-one, it makes eight years of schooling and five of residency delayed."

I thought about it for a second and asked, "But then you'd only be thirty-six." I let my statement hang in the air, and he pressed his lips into a line as if he didn't want to respond, but he coughed up an answer as he moved toward the couch.

"Well, it would have been perfect if my marriage wouldn't have been what it was. Add to that a child, and well, life got in the way." He slumped onto the couch, and I thought of how my delayed start had me starting my residency only one year earlier than his. It wasn't all bad. He knew what he wanted and he was being successful. And being older while learning probably was what had given him the edge he had, what had made him that much more successful than the other residents in his rotation.

"Would it be so bad?" I asked, sitting gingerly next to him on the couch. I placed the book on the coffee table next to his laptop and angled my body to face him.

"Would what be bad?" he asked, seeming confused. So I helped him out.

"If there was a spark here." I pointed to him, then to myself. "If we hit it off. If we found that we have a lot in common and we like each other."

I'd been waiting to ask that all evening. I thoroughly enjoyed every second I spent with him now, especially when his daughter was around. He was kind and compassionate, despite my first impression of his being stodgy and a bit cocky. In fact, he wasn't at all cocky or braggadocious. He was humble and confident.

"Think about your studies, Sophia." My name on his lips was heaven. He hadn't said it in ten days, and I was aching to hear it. It soothed a deep need in my mind. "You'll be distracted. The board and HR will hound us. We'd have to sneak around. It would cause problems at work. We just can't."

"Jack, I've never felt a connection like this with anyone in my life. You're easy to talk to. You know what I'm going to say before I say it. We have all the same interests and hobbies, yet we're both independent enough to not demand each other's attention. It makes sense. I know you feel it too." My body felt on edge all of a sudden, hoping he didn't react negatively. Rejection would suck so badly.

"Sophia, you're right. I feel it, but I know hospital policy, and I am in the middle of this messy custody thing. I just don't have the wavelength to do this." The way he said that only made me want him more, to help him with the custody thing, to give him the capacity to open himself for how amazing this could be.

"No one has to know. We can be super professional and if something develops, I can have my father get me an internship somewhere else. Or if it works out, we can just keep it a secret." I inched closer to him on the couch, and he seemed to notice but didn't shy away.

"And when one or both of us lose our job? What about my ex?" His eyebrows rose, but I still wasn't deterred.

"Let's give her something to talk about," I told him, rising up to come closer. I knelt on either side of his hips and straddled him, this time much more comfortably than in his office. "Judges like a dad who moves on and finds a good woman to be a role model for their daughter."

I had no idea if that was true, but at that point I'd have done just about anything to convince him. The need growing inside me was consuming me like a forest fire.

Jack's hands rested on my hips and he asked, "Are you sure you're willing to take the risk?"

"No risk, no reward." I leaned down and kissed him softly. At first he was hesitant and the kiss was shallow, but when I rocked my hips, he seemed to get the point that I wasn't going to back down. If I could stand up to my father and refuse to leave this city just so I could see if Jack and I had what it took to do this, I could definitely make my desires for him known.

Jack's hands became greedy and impetuous, taking their liberty across my body while I held his face in my hands and kissed him hard. When he gripped me by the ass and pinned my body against his as he stood, I gasped and shrieked quietly.

"Shh, unless you want this ruined by a curious seven-year-old." His hiss was caution enough. I wrapped my arms and legs around him as he carried me into the dark hallway. The kissing continued as he burst into a room and shut the door behind him. He dropped me on the bed and then returned to lock the door and turn the light on.

His room was average sized, but he had a king-size bed, upon which I was sprawled. Jack returned to disrobe me in under twenty seconds as his hungry lips placed fiery kisses everywhere he bared my body. I tore his clothes off equally as fast, but he managed to snag his wallet out of his back pocket and produce a foil-wrapped condom.

"Not planning on that happening again, huh?" I asked. After the last time and no condom, with the mishap I had even come prepared, though the condom I brought was in the living room in the recliner where I dropped my purse.

"You know what? You keep being snarky like that and I'll tie you up so I can have my way with you." He smirked at me as he dropped the condom on the bed next to me and crawled across my body.

"I think I can live with that," I purred as he started nipping along my throat and collarbone. "Is that a challenge, Mister?" His mouth attacked my neck, sucking, biting, and licking. Everywhere he went, a trail of fire followed him. I couldn't wait for him to stop teasing me and just take me already.

"Oh, Honey, you have no idea," he growled against my ear before claiming my lips with his own again.

"Shit," I managed to gasp out between kisses. He kissed his way down my body, stopping at my breasts and then continuing southward until he reached my core. His hands gripped the backs of my thighs and he pushed until my body slid upward on the bed. Then he dived in, lapping at my silken folds, sucking and nipping my sensitive skin. "Ooh." My moan was probably a bit louder than it should have been, but I caught myself and laced my fingers in his hair as he devoured me.

Jack placed two fingers inside me, curling them upward, searching for that spot which he knew would make me scream his name. He found it, and I bucked my hips against his mouth and his fingers, moaning louder this time. He slipped in a third finger, stretching me, preparing me for what was to come. I whimpered and clenched, and he started thrusting his fingers. All I could do was claw his scalp and hang on for the ride as his tongue circled my clit and drove me wild.

"Fuck, Jack!" I screamed as he sucked me into a mind-blowing orgasm. I convulsed and writhed, forgetting my grip on his hair as I grabbed one of my tits and squeezed while I clawed at the mattress below me. He continued his movements until I was shaking and spent, then he crawled over me.

"Condom," I managed to mutter, but he was already on it, tearing it open with his mouth and rolling it onto his rock-hard dick.

He grabbed my thighs again, and with one swift motion, he entered me, filling me to the hilt. We both groaned in unison, savoring the overdue reunion of our bodies. He started off slow, kissing me deeply while thrusting in and out, his tempo increasing desire by desire. I wrapped my legs around his waist and met every thrust he gave me, moaning into his mouth.

I could taste myself on his tongue, the sweet yet savory flavor of my juices coating his lips and chin.

He growled and picked up the pace, slamming into me over and over, his body slapping against mine. My back arched with every thrust, my fingernails digging into his shoulders as pleasure built deep inside me.

"Fuck, Jack, I'm gonna..." I panted, barely able to speak coherent sentences.

"Squeeze that hot little pussy around me," he managed to grunt out before he tilted my hips upward and drove himself even deeper into me than I thought possible. He hit that spot again, sending me over the edge into another intense orgasm.

"Oh, God, Jack... Yes!" I whimpered out as quietly as I could. He continued to pound in and out of me, his own release imminent. His face contorted with ecstasy, and a second later he joined me in climax, slowing his thrusts then collapsing on top of me in a sweaty heap.

The relaxation that sank into my body was sheer bliss. I hardly noticed when he rolled out of bed to remove the condom, but there was no mistaking his intention when he came back and pulled me to his side of the bed and held me, then covered my body.

"I should..." I reached as if I were trying to get up, and he held me more tightly.

"Stay," he whispered, then he nipped my ear. I had a feeling this could be a long night. I sank back onto the bed and let him wrap himself around me as his hand slid between my legs and rubbed.

I had to be assertive more often. I liked what it got me.

16

JACK

It was an odd but pleasant sensation, sharing my bed with a woman again after so long. There had been several nights over the past few years where Leah sought comfort by climbing up next to me during a thunderstorm or after having had a nightmare, but otherwise, I'd had this whole king-size bed to myself.

Last night, I lay curled around Sophia's body for the large part, except when she woke to use the toilet and came back, whereupon she held me briefly. I woke slowly, listening to the sound of her light snoring and trying to wrap my mind around what was actually happening.

We'd had a few brief conversations about why this entire situation was a bad idea—the hospital policy, our distractedness, the way others might perceive us, including my ex-wife. But none of those rationalizations seemed to stand up to the immense chemistry we had when we got together. And last night when Sophia asked me if it would be so bad if we leaned into the chemistry and connection, I just lost it.

Life hadn't been easy for me. It had been one struggle after another, and I credited my persistence and determination, as well as ambition and drive, to that struggle. They say what doesn't kill you makes you stronger, and I was living proof that statement was true. If I had been a weaker man, I would have given up years ago.

So when such a treasure like Sophia came along, I couldn't resist rewarding myself for all my hard work and consoling myself after all the difficulties I'd endured. It was wrong of me. I knew that much. But I had no self-control around her. She was the kindling, and the raging forest fire inside me needed to devour her.

I pulled her against my body and breathed in the scent of her auburn hair, sweet, floral hints. It was so much more than just a guilty pleasure, however. Sophia felt like the missing half of my soul that I'd been searching for my entire life. She fit me in ways Dana never had, like our shared passion for medicine and helping others. Or the fact that we could talk for hours about anything and not grow bored of one another.

With Dana, I had never been able to sustain a conversation about anything that interested me. She'd have turned to her phone or book, whatever it was she was doing. Though, when we discussed her hobbies and interests, she engaged wholeheartedly. It was that way with a lot of things, and while I could discuss book club and shopping deals for a while, there was only so much I could give without needing to be refilled myself.

"Mmm," Sophia moaned, and her chest rose in a deep breath. A smile formed on her lips before she even opened her eyes and then she rolled to her back. I scooted backward, allowing her some space, and she reached up and pecked me on the jaw. "Good morning," she purred. Her eyes blinked open slowly and she kept the same sweet smile as she yawned.

"Morning, beautiful. How did you sleep?" My hand rested on her stomach, though I itched to feel her skin against mine. We had agreed in the wee hours of the morning when we finally lay down that it was best for both of us to have clothing on in case Leah woke in the night and needed me. Sophia wore one of my large T-shirts and her panties, and I slept in gym shorts like normal.

"I haven't slept that well in years."

I wanted to tell her that I hadn't either, but a light tap on my door announced Leah's arrival. Normally on a Saturday morning, she would wake me for breakfast of French toast or pancakes. On occasion, I'd surprise her and wake her up to go out and get donuts and chocolate milk, but today we had company. In the split second it took her to turn the knob and open the door, I started to second-guess my decision to have Sophia stay with me.

Leah had been exposed to God only knows how many men Dana had brought home, and at the park, she had made it very clear how much she disliked that. While Sophia and I weren't exactly dating, and thus she'd never slept over before, Leah had been happy enough to spend time with her. But what would my little girl think if she knew we were more than just friends? And how was I supposed to tell her that?

"Daddy?" she called, and her sleepy face appeared around the corner of the door. Her eyebrows rose, and Sophia rolled back onto her side to face the doorway.

"Hey, squirt, good morning," Sophia said, and I heard the affection in her tone. My heart warmed to the idea of this being a reality while simultaneously tensing in preparation for Leah to buck at the idea. All children wanted their parents to get back together after a divorce. Leah would probably feel the same way.

"Sophia!" Leah cheered, and without warning, she raced across the room and leapt up onto the bed, shaking the whole thing and climbing on Sophia.

"Whoa," I chided, wondering how Sophia would take it, but she simply wrapped Leah up in her arms and turned over until my daughter was between our bodies on the bed. We were beneath the covers and Leah was on top of them, and she was all smiles.

"Daddy, you didn't tell me you were having a sleepover." Leah's admonishment was playful but serious at the same time. "I could have stayed up later." She crossed her arms over her chest, and Sophia tickled her, which made Leah giggle and squirm.

"Grownup sleepovers are boring. You didn't miss anything, except more studying and a bit of exercise." Sophia winked at me, and I chuckled at how she called our sexual exploits "exercise". It was an honest way of making sex sound very boring, indeed.

"I hate exercise, blech!" Leah stuck her tongue out and pointed into her mouth as if she were retching, then she turned over and sat up. "Can we play that video game?"

My daughter's quick acceptance of another woman in my bed made me feel less anxious on that front, but suddenly very anxious on another. What was happening between me and Sophia really shouldn't have been happening. It was a major risk for work, and I knew exactly how much she distracted me. She may have been more on top of her game, but to me I had to focus much harder to concentrate on work and not let her nearness get to me.

When this whole thing blew up—and it would—would Leah get caught in the crossfire? Would she be too attached to Sophia and have her heart broken? Was I rushing into things and not thinking carefully about the repercussions to other people who may be affected by this? It went beyond potentially losing my job or being reprimanded. I could hurt my little girl's heart.

"How about we have a yummy breakfast first? If Daddy has the things, I'll make us pancakes." Sophia turned to look at me, and I snapped out of my spiraling thoughts. She was so good with kids, and I felt like a big, dumb oaf sometimes. Leah needed a nurturing mother figure because as a man I fell short, and Dana was anything but nurturing. Sophia was so good for my little girl, which made my heart lean back toward loving more things about the beautiful intern.

"Yeah, I have the stuff," I told her, but as the girls celebrated and cheered, I remembered how young Sophia was.

"Let's go!" Leah called, and she crawled across the bed and climbed off.

"Be there in a second," Sophia told her, and Leah raced out.

I admired how good Sophia was with my little girl, but I wondered if that would ever be enough for her. Sophia was still of childbearing age, still probably had hopes of being a mother, and I was almost forty. Leah was already seven, but by the time she was an adult, I'd be pushing fifty and ready to retire. I couldn't imagine starting over again at this age, and if Sophia wanted more kids, it would be a disappointment to her.

"Gonna go make pancakes. Want some?" she asked, kissing me on the cheek.

"Yeah, sure," I told her, then I watched as she went to my dresser with confidence and pulled out a pair of shorts and put them on. One night in my house and she acted like she owned the place, and I was the one who made her feel that comfortable. I wasn't sure if I was that comfortable yet.

Sophia slipped out, and I lay there for a second toiling over what was going on. I had told Sophia we would give it a shot, but there was so much riding on my shoulders I didn't know if I had the capacity to handle this. I didn't know if the added worry and complications outweighed the pleasure I drew from taking this risk, or if it was worth it.

One thing I did know was Sophia made me feel things and come alive in ways I had never experienced. Russian roulette was a dangerous game, and I'd already spun the cylinder. I was just nervous to pull the trigger.

17

SOPHIA

The steady beep of the heart monitor filled the OR, a soft background hum to the tension in the air. I adjusted my grip on the suction device, keeping the field clear as Jack worked. My hands were steady, more so than usual, and I wasn't sure if it was from practice or something else.

Jack's voice cut through the room, calm and controlled. "Dr. Chen, keep the suction on the junction. This isn't the time to lose focus." His words were a chastisement, but even still, they weren't harsh. Not the way he spoke to Dr. Briggs. I knew the past few weeks of our sneaking around, stealing kisses, was the reason. He had a soft spot for me.

"I'm on it," I said, a little too quickly, trying to sound as composed as he did. God, why was I so keyed-up today? I'd assisted him dozens of times by now, but today felt different. Maybe it was the surgery, because Dr. Briggs was in here with us. Or maybe it was the fact that we had spent the last two nights together, and I still hadn't figured out how to act around him when we were surrounded by a sterile field and a heart monitor instead of... well, each other.

Focus, Sophie, focus. My mind scolded itself, and I blinked hard to push away the distracting thoughts.

The surgery wasn't anything wildly complicated—at least, not for Jack. The patient had a rare thoracic vascular malformation that required precision, but we weren't in crisis mode. Not yet, at least. Jack made it look easy, his hands moving with that effortless skill that still left me in awe sometimes. I knew I was in the right place learning from the right doctor, even if my dad didn't agree.

And then there was me, trying not to remember the way those hands had felt just two nights ago, tracing over my skin with the same kind of practiced care. My God, was he incredible. Not the time to think about that. Definitely not.

"Dr. Briggs, pass me the clamp," Jack said, breaking into my thoughts. Dr. Briggs handed him the instrument, a little too quickly. His nerves were showing. He was far more practiced than me, but anything out of the routine appendectomy or gallbladder surgery had him shaken, the way I used to feel every time I walked into this place.

Jack glanced over at my co-intern but didn't say anything. He was too focused on the delicate work in front of us. The clamp secured a small vessel that'd been threatening to cause trouble, and I felt a rush of relief. He was always steady under pressure. Me? I was getting better at it—mostly thanks to him.

Dr. Briggs, though, was still learning. He'd been watching me the whole time, probably noticing how different I was today. I could feel it myself—my movements more sure, my focus sharper, like I had something to prove, because I did. Or maybe it wasn't about proving anything. Maybe it was just that being around Jack had started to feel like second nature. Too natural, actually. And too intimate.

"Dr. Chen," Jack said, his tone a little softer than before. I snapped my gaze up to him. "Keep an eye on the junction here. We can't afford a bleed."

"I've got it," I replied, my voice steady, though my heart wasn't. There it was again—his voice—that calm, confident tone that did something to me. God, I needed to get my head together. He wasn't thinking about anything but the surgery. He never lost focus like I did. Not here, at least.

"Dr. Chen, you seem... different today," Dr. Briggs said, almost too casually.

I froze for a second, feeling heat rise to my cheeks, even under the mask. Jack didn't respond, his attention still fixed on the surgical field. I wasn't about to respond either, but Dr. Briggs didn't seem to get the memo.

"I mean, not in a bad way," Dr. Briggs continued, oblivious. "You just seem... I don't know, more confident."

I could feel Jack's eyes flick to me for a split second before he went back to work, and my stomach did a strange little flip. I knew how he felt, how he'd already cautioned me that I was changing and blossoming into a confident doctor. I was supposed to, after all, but he warned me how our secret escapades could result in my making mistakes. The reason I had to try even harder to focus on what I was doing and couldn't afford distractions like Dr. Briggs was bringing up right now.

"Well, when you work with the same person enough, you start to find your rhythm," I told him, trying to keep my tone casual. I wasn't going to let Dr. Briggs' curiosity pull me into anything I didn't want to reveal.

"Uh-huh," Dr. Briggs said, clearly unconvinced.

Dr. Thornton cut in before I could respond. "Dr. Briggs, pay attention to the vitals, not the conversation."

The way Jack's voice shifted told me he wasn't in the mood for small talk, but there was something else in his tone. Maybe I was imagining it, but there was a tension there, something barely concealed. Or maybe I was just projecting. The harsh tone of his voice resembled my first day when he told me I wasn't here to play guessing games. And the wince on Dr. Briggs's face showed how much he disliked being chastised.

I went back to my task, focusing on the suction. I felt Jack's gaze on me again, brief but intense. We had worked together a lot in the last five weeks, but this was different. This wasn't just about being good in the OR. He looked at me like his lover, another warning to conceal the intimacy we shared, and I had tried to do just that.

But now it was starting to show.

The heart monitor gave a sudden beep, sharp and jarring.

"Dr. Thornton," I said, trying to keep my voice level. It felt jarring to use his title. His hands stilled, and I could see the subtle change in his posture.

"I see it," Jack replied, his voice as calm as ever, but I could feel the shift in the room. "Dr. Chen, keep that suction in place. Dr. Briggs, check the pressure."

Dr. Briggs fumbled with the monitor, his hands a little shaky. I could almost feel his panic rising, but Jack wasn't rattled. Not even close.

"The pressure's dropping," Dr. Briggs said, his voice tight. "What do we do?"

"We don't panic," Jack replied smoothly, his hands moving faster now, working with a precision that took my breath away. "Dr. Chen, stay with me. We've got a vessel leak."

I nodded, feeling that familiar rush of adrenaline as I adjusted the suction, keeping the area as clear as I could. We'd done this before—worked together through tough moments—and somehow, we always clicked.

Jack moved quickly, tying off the vessel in what felt like record time. I was holding my breath, watching him the whole time, and when he finally leaned back, I realized I hadn't exhaled in what felt like forever.

"Pressure's stabilizing," Dr. Briggs announced, his voice shaky but relieved. "We're good."

Jack glanced up at me, and for a moment, it was just the two of us. His eyes held mine, and I knew he was thinking the same thing I was. We were like two cogs in a well-oiled machine.

I looked away first, my pulse still racing, but not from the surgery.

Dr. Briggs cleared his throat, bringing me back to the present. "You two really have a rhythm, huh?" He sounded curious but a little suspicious.

I forced a smile behind my mask, trying to shrug it off. "Yeah, I guess we do."

Jack didn't say anything, just gave a quick nod. He handed me the final instrument to close the incision. My hands moved on autopilot, but my mind wasn't in the OR anymore. It was back to the nights we'd spent together, the quiet moments between shifts that no one else knew about.

When I tied off the last suture, I glanced up again, catching Jack's gaze again. There was something in his eyes, something no one else would notice but me. It was a reminder of what we weren't saying out loud.

"Good work, Dr. Chen," Jack said with a steady voice, but I could hear the edge to it—the tension beneath the professionalism. I wondered if Dr. Briggs heard it too.

But if he did, he didn't say anything. He just watched as I finished, probably still wondering exactly what had changed between me and Jack.

Dr. Briggs was the first to leave and scrub out. The nursing staff stayed to finish the dressing and clean up along with the anesthesiologist. Jack and I made our way out of the OR just as Dr. Briggs was leaving the scrub room. He'd be in Jack's office when we got there, so we only had a split second of privacy. But Jack stole a kiss and grabbed my ass with a firm grip, leaving a bloody handprint on my surgical gown which I quickly tore off and tossed in the bin.

"Now, Dr. Thornton, you're going to get caught if you keep being risky like that." I smirked at him as I took off my gloves then stripped off my mask.

He was disrobing too, prepping to wash his hands and go back to his office for a debrief about the surgery. I thought it went well, and I'd have guessed Jack did too. Except with Dr. Briggs's suspicious behavior, I knew later tonight there would be another serious conversation. We'd had so many of them that I already rehearsed in my mind what he'd tell me, that we were walking on thin ice, dangling by a thread. That he had to keep his job.

I loved that he was so cautious and protective of both his job and mine, but I knew he was being too worried. Even if Dr. Briggs came right out and accused us of having an affair, he had no proof.

"Well if you don't stop being so fucking amazing in the OR, you're going to give it away. Briggs is getting jealous of you." Jack winked at me and turned on the faucet. I stood beside him washing my hands and feeling giddy about the closeness I felt with him.

"You think he's just jealous? I felt like he was suspicious."

"He might be. We just have to be more careful." Jack seemed too casual for this moment, but maybe he was feeling more relaxed and at ease with me too. "See you in my office," he said, pecking me on the cheek quickly before grabbing a towel and darting out.

I finished up and started toward his office when I got a phone call. My cell, buried in my pants pocket, vibrated against my leg, so I stopped to pull it out and answer.

"Dr. Chen speaking. How can I help you?" This number was only for professional calls, though my parents had it for emergencies. My personal cell was in my locker in the doctors' lounge. I didn't know who would even call me here since I wasn't on call, but a call was a call.

"Dr. Chen, this is Dr. Manning from Johns Hopkins. Is now a good time?" The man's voice paralyzed me. I stood stock still in the hallway, staring at Jack's back as he disappeared from view down the way.

"Uh, hi. Yes, it's okay." I went from bold, confident Sophia to anxious and indecisive Sophia instantly. My father had given this man my number without my permission and I didn't know how to respond to that. He clearly had not listened to my words when I told him I was happy here and not planning to leave.

"Dr. Chen, I was informed by your father that you are looking to upgrade your residency. Is this correct?" The man paused, but I couldn't even stammer out a sentence before he continued. "It was quite a feat, but I have secured a grant to allow me to take on one more intern this year, with an allowance in the budget to extend the offer for up to five years total. Now this would be a localized trauma surgeon residency, not the generalized surgical you're doing now, but I believe it is worth your while. The pay is better, and for the time spent, you'll have more experience."

I stuttered out a few syllables and felt like crying. Anger rose up and swelled in my chest until my eyes were tearing up. Dad had no right to do this. He knew how easily I was pushed around and swayed by other people. He'd done something similar when I wanted to join marching band and I was determined to play clarinet, and he told the band director I wanted to play trumpet—because it was more practical. Needless to say, I ended up cowering and playing the brass instead of woodwinds.

"Dr. Manning, can I please get back with you on this?" I asked, not even knowing where to begin with him. I couldn't just outright refuse. I'd look like a complete idiot. My father was the respected one, not me. They'd think I was being selfish and insubordinate, which I was, but only because I should have been allowed to make my own choices.

"Certainly, but think quickly. We only have this availability for four weeks to make the decision, and I have to provide the option for a few other interns too, just in case." Dr. Manning sounded like a very nice man, but he wasn't Jack, and he wasn't my first choice.

"Thank you," I told him, and I hung up with shaking hands. I knew if Dr. Briggs found out that I'd been offered such an incredible internship at such a prestigious hospital whose reputation outweighed Twin Peaks' by miles, he would know something was up. No one would stay here instead of taking that offer. No one but me.

And I only had one singular reason for staying. And it wasn't the medicine.

18

JACK

The car bumped along the road and Sophia's hand rested on top of mine on the shifter. We were headed across town where the likelihood of anyone recognizing us was slim so we could have dinner out. I was set to pick up Leah later, when dinner was over, because Sophia promised to make a blanket fort and have a sleepover with her. I thought it was sweet, especially given how well the two were bonding. After four weeks of Sophia and me sneaking around and Leah knowing about it, it was about time we let her get involved.

"Wow, that's a lot of flashing lights," Sophia said, noticing the same thing I had. Traffic was already heavy, even on the highway, and we'd seen three cop cars, a fire truck, and an ambulance since we got into the car at my place ten minutes ago. It wasn't abnormal for something like this to happen when there was a bad accident, but being a surgeon, I was always on alert.

"Yeah, I hope it's not bad. It's on the east side of the city, though, so we should be good." Neither one of us were on call for this weekend either, which meant even if it was something that was emergent, we wouldn't be called in.

The light turned green and I pulled away, watching two more sets of flashing lights flash through the intersection in my rearview mirror. It made me sigh with discouragement because I knew that big of a response meant whatever hospital they took crash victims to would have their hands full.

"Hey," Sophia soothed, rubbing my bicep, "let's just enjoy dinner. Okay?" Her soft features drew me in. There was no way for me to stay worried or distracted for long when she was around.

"You're right." I turned on Fifth Street toward the restaurant and turned my hand over. She laced her fingers through mine, and I noticed from the corner of my eye that she smiled.

"I can't wait for the sleepover," she said, and my dick tingled.

"Me either," I said in a very suggestive tone. I wagged my eyebrows and pictured her naked and draped across my bed. More and more, I was enjoying fucking her brains out and then talking for hours afterward.

"I mean with Leah." She swatted my arm and chuckled. "I haven't done anything fun like this in decades. I was too old after I turned twelve, or at least my parents said so. I was forced into music lessons and dance, tutoring, sports... Anything but imaginative fun. I am really looking forward to just building a fort, eating popcorn, watching a princess movie, and painting my nails."

When I glanced at her, I noticed how happy and content she seemed, though her eyes betrayed a bit of fatigue. It had been a rough week for us with surgeries back-to-back most days. I hoped her energy level stayed elevated long enough to deal with a feisty seven-year-old.

"You really like hanging out with Leah, don't you?" I couldn't keep staring at her, so I had to rely on her words and the tone of her voice to communicate, but I knew she'd never lie.

"I think I love that little girl to pieces, Jack." Sophia rested her head on my shoulder across the center console and my heart warmed. "I mean it when I say how sweet she is. I love spending time with her. It makes me realize how much I will love being a mother someday."

The sweet sigh at the end of her statement made me smile, but my body felt tense too. It was one of the things we had to discuss, because there was no point in continuing a relationship, no matter how well we clicked emotionally, if our life goals weren't matched up. I wasn't sure about having more kids so late in life. And being ten years younger than me, I knew she had her whole life ahead of her.

I opened my mouth to respond, hoping maybe to break the ice on that topic in general, when my phone rang through my speakers. I pressed the hands-free button on my steering wheel and glanced at the screen. It was Twin Peaks.

"Shit," I hissed under my breath before saying, "Hello, Jack Thornton here."

"Jack, uh… Dr. Thornton, it's Rita at Twin Peaks. We need you to come in. There was a building collapse across town. They're at max capacity already with dozens more people injured. Some of these folks need a surgeon, buddy." Rita sounded flustered and busy, and I glanced at Sophia and noted the disappointment on her face. She frowned but nodded, and I knew I had to respond.

"What's the ETA on the buses? How many? What am I looking at?" I turned at the next intersection, heading back toward the highway. My black suit and Sophia's cute blue dress would be completely out of place under scrubs, but we had no choice. And I needed her help.

"We have at least five buses coming on diversion, with who knows how many more. Right now we're looking at a tension pneumothorax and a perforated colon. We suspect a ruptured spleen on that one." Rita rattled off the list of injuries highest in priority but continued for thirty more seconds with a rundown of less life-threatening injuries, including a broken leg that needed set and a partially severed limb, which could have a tourniquet while we fixed up our near-death patients.

I had to pull my hand away from Sophia's and focus on the road. My mind switched gears from distracted lover to skilled surgeon easily, and Sophia seemed to take the hint. She started removing her earrings and the hairpins out of her fancy up-do, and I watched her tie her hair up in a knot.

"I'll be there in twelve minutes flat. Have an OR prepped for the TPX right away. If that bus is there in twenty minutes, I want that OR ready in nineteen. Got it?" My mind raced with possibilities and I was already rehearsing the incisions and insertion of the chest tube in my head.

"Got it. See you soon." Rita hung up, and I was immediately apologetic.

"I'm so sorry, Soph. I know how much you were looking forward to this." I drove like a bat straight out of hell and didn't care if I got blueberries and cherries behind me. They'd have to take it up with the hospital and the dying patients. Besides, the focus was probably on the building collapse across town. I knew it was bad when we'd seen so many first responder vehicles. I just didn't think it would come to this.

"Just drive, Jack. People need our help." Sophia's shift from my lover to my intern was just as immediate as mine, and I felt strangely calmed by that.

As we drove, she started walking through the steps of the surgeries we had to do audibly and I knew she was on the ball. They'd have called in the other surgeons by now, the on-call doctor and even Dr. Briggs. For an emergency this large, every available medically trained person would be on duty, like it or not.

We squealed into the parking lot a full ninety seconds sooner than I planned and I slammed the car into park while I said, "Stay in the car. Wait two minutes, then walk in after me. They can't see us arrive together all dressed up like this. Go straight to trauma one and scrub in." I opened the door then turned back and leaned across the center console and kissed her briefly. "And lock up the car, bring me my keys. And get your Crocs. It could be a long night."

Even in the rush to get to my patient, I was thinking about her comfort. Those spiked patent-leather heels would kill her feet after a while.

Darting toward the hospital, I took my phone out of my pocket and called Dana. If things were as bad as they seemed, it meant I wouldn't be getting Leah tonight, after all. That would definitely piss my ex-wife off, but it couldn't be avoided. It rang several times before anyone picked up and I was already in the heart of the emergency department when they finally did.

"My God, Jack, don't tell me you're going to fucking cancel on me again." Dana sounded furious, but I didn't know what to tell her. When I signed up for this job, I knew it meant being prepared at a minute's notice to help, and here I was. You'd have thought being a first responder would give me more honor, not this bullshit.

"Dana, there was a building collapse. I'm going in to the hospital." I didn't have to explain, or at least, I shouldn't have had to explain. This was my job and people depended on me.

"I have plans, Jack. You can't just dump Leah on me last-minute. What kind of father are you?"

The selfishness of that statement infuriated me, but I was a trained professional and I had to keep my calm. I couldn't let her rile me up any more than I could let Sophia get me worked up sexually. People's lives were at stake.

"Look, I'm just telling you what's happening. I can't help it. I have to perform life-saving surgery. Leah will understand. I can pick her up first thing in the morning." I walked past Rita with the phone pinched between my ear and shoulder as I undid my cufflinks and headed for the doctors' lounge where I could find my scrubs and scrub cap. Rita gave me a thumbs-up, and I nodded as she indicated seven minutes left.

"You mean while I'm sleeping in? You're ridiculous."

"I have to go, Dana. I'll call you in the morning." I let the phone drop to my hand and continued walking, but the last thing I heard her say was so cruel.

"We'll see if a judge agrees with me that you spend no time with your daughter." I knew she was so mad about this, but her anger was misplaced.

No one liked to have their plans rearranged, and these types of situations were disappointing. But I put myself in the shoes of the victims or their families and how they would look to doctors and nurses with hope and desperation. I wished Dana would be more like me, holding a space in her heart for those who were hurting, even through discouragement. I wished she'd be more like Sophia.

Ten minutes later, Sophia and I were walking into the operating room, scrubbed in and ready to do the chest tube. The patient's vitals were all over the place and he was screaming in pain. I had the team sedate him and we got to work. It took thirty minutes to place the tube and position it correctly, then tape it in place. We waited another fifteen for the pressure to start alleviating and the air to begin abating. It was touch and go, but when his vitals started to level out, I knew we were out of the most dangerous part.

It might take as much as three days for his lung to fully inflate and stay that way, but his heart was no longer under the extreme duress. The other doctors could tend to his multiple lacerations and broken bones, but he would live.

I gave Sophia a nod of appreciation for her stellar attitude under such pressure. She had been the steady, consistent help I needed, though a trained perioperative nurse may also have done the same, but not the way Sophia did. She and I worked together so well, I was ashamed to admit I knew I'd be less of a surgeon when she finally moved on to her own practice and I had to do it alone again. It'd be hard to find another assistant like her.

"Touch and go for a minute there," she said as she scrubbed out. We had less than ten minutes to get to the next OR for the next patient. Dr. Briggs and his supervisor had taken the perforated bowel, which left us with a mild case of internal bleeding which needed a surgeon's keen eye.

"I'm proud of you. After that emergency a few weeks ago, I worried you'd feel too overwhelmed again." I knew how easily Sophia got flustered and how much she cared about her patients. It wasn't a dig, just a cautious and compassionate observation.

"I feel better now with you around, though I feel nauseous." She pressed a hand to her stomach and closed her eyes for a second, then returned to scrubbing. Her fatigue and now this nausea concerned me. She'd been working so hard, and I knew how easy it was to get burned out early in your career.

"Maybe you should go home. You're not required to be here, you know? I can handle this." I knew I could, but I didn't want to do it alone. She was part of my team now and I relied on her help.

"Are you kidding? And skip this excitement? What stories would I tell my grandkids someday?" She winked at me, but her face looked a little green. "Did you call your ex? How did Leah take the news?"

I reached for a towel and scowled. "Dana never lets me speak to her, so I don't know. What I know is she threatened me again, and I'm not taking kindly to it. She thinks she's more important than the whole world. I just don't know what to do."

"*Dr. Thornton, OR Six is prepped.*" The loudspeaker announcement interrupted my thoughts, and I was glad. I couldn't let myself dive off into the deep end of anger.

"Let's get going. We have to scrub in next door." I nodded at the door and left ahead of Sophia, but I knew she'd follow. I just hoped her nauseous stomach wasn't my fault. She hadn't even eaten dinner yet. I owed her, big time.

19

SOPHIA

The heat of Jack's kisses left my lips as he rolled away from my body, leaving me panting and exhausted. My sweat-slicked skin started to cool as my heart rate slowly came back down to a normal rhythm. My body felt heavy and relaxed as endorphins continued pulsing through every muscle fiber.

Jack was so good at that, making me have explosive orgasms, and I was putty in his hands. He climbed out of bed to dispose of the condom, and I felt the entire mattress shake. I let my eyes flutter shut and just enjoyed the afterglow until he returned to my side and pulled me against himself. He was hot too, panting, and he pressed a kiss to my temple before pulling a sweaty ringlet from my skin and tucking it behind my ear.

"Have I ever told you how incredible you are?" Jack had a lot more scruff than usual this morning, and my nether region was feeling it. I was almost raw from his generous acts of service between my thighs, and I grinned as he kissed me and I tasted my moisture on his lips.

"I think once or twice," I moaned, rolling into his chest.

"I've been thinking." He sighed contentedly and kissed my forehead a few times. It was like he hadn't kissed anyone in years, like he couldn't get enough of kissing me.

"What about?" I asked, tracing lazy figure-eights on his chest. He was damp with sweat too, and I wondered if he'd shower with me if I asked him to.

I'd spent the whole weekend with him and we had to head into work in a little more than an hour, barring any emergencies that called us in sooner. After last week's building collapse, we'd been given stand-down time regarding our on-call hours. I was glad for the bit of free time, but I had spent it all with Jack, not at home studying the way my parents would have liked.

"About us." Jack's voice was so wistful and dreamy, like he was happy and content with me, and that made me feel happier and more content with him too.

What we were doing, sneaking around for sex, was wrong on so many levels, but we'd managed to make it work for us. No one at the hospital was suspicious of our relationship, and even Dr. Briggs stopped questioning how seamlessly Jack and I worked together now. We were able to concentrate and do our jobs well, and this intimate connection with him gave me just the confidence I needed to perform at my highest level of skill.

"Yeah?" I brushed my lips over his chest and felt his chest hair tickle my nose. The throbbing between my legs was slowly subsiding, and I was already craving the nearness again. Jack did things to me I couldn't explain, things I wanted to feel forever.

"Yeah," he said, then he curled a few more strands of hair behind my ear. "I am. I think we should go to HR. I want to declare our relationship, Soph." He'd started using that pet name for me when we were alone, and I liked it. It was like taking our relationship to the next level somehow.

But this? What he was saying now? It had me instantly feeling tense and hesitant. "Why do we need to do that?" I didn't want him to think I wasn't ready for a relationship. My God, was I ever ready. I was falling in love with every part of him, and I had even imagined what life would be like if I lived here, if Leah started to call me Mom. He and I were so right for each other, and I hoped that he felt the same way.

"Well, it's the right thing. I looked into it... went back and read the employee manual online. It turns out there's an allowance for two employees to date each other. They just have to declare the relationship and fill out the paperwork. There'd be some fuss about time off if we were both to request the same days too often, but in all, it's a pathway forward to the next step for us." He smiled and pulled back so we could look each other in the eye.

"So, that's it? We just tell them and we're good?" I felt tense, my stomach rolling around inside my body the way it had been for days now. It had me a bit worried that our little oopsie seven weeks ago was more than an oopsie, but I hadn't said anything to Jack yet. Not until I was sure.

"Well, that's not all." He grimaced and looked down, avoiding my eyes. "They'd end up moving you to a different department. You wouldn't be able to finish your residency with me. But we'd have each other. We could continue this." His hand touched under the bottom of my chin, and he met my gaze again, but I felt tears welling up.

I'd also been so emotional and tired the past few weeks too, which also wasn't a good sign. But I blinked back the tears this time because I didn't want him to start asking questions.

"Jack, I can't do that." I shook my head and sat up, deciding that a shower wasn't going to happen. The close intimacy I felt was now clouded with fear. "My parents... They already think this is a bad idea. My dad knows too many people. If he finds out I was moved from one department to another, he'll ask questions. He'll figure out it's because I'm dating you. He'll force me to go to Maryland."

I started collecting my clothing from the various places on the carpet where they fell last night when Jack wrestled them off me, and I got dressed while Jack watched.

"Alright, I understand, but won't they have to find out about us sometime anyway?" He sounded hurt, and that wasn't my goal.

I turned and frowned at him. "I'm not trying to keep you a secret, Jack. I'm trying to keep my parents happy so I don't incur their wrath. You don't know them. Honor is a huge thing in my dad's culture. Just by staying at Twin Peaks, I'm rebelling against his wishes. Being booted from the residency I've fought so hard to keep would destroy me." My lip quivered, and I thought I'd throw up.

"Alright," he said, climbing back out of the bed. He came to me and gripped my neck softly with both hands, thumbs on my jaw. He kissed my lips tenderly, but I could see the disappointment in his eyes. "I understand."

"I have to go. I need to stop somewhere on the way home before I get to work." That somewhere was a place I had no intention of telling him about, but I knew it was time. I'd spent several mornings praying to the porcelain goddess, and my body was utterly exhausted by the schedule I had to keep.

"Sure, I'll see you there." Jack pulled away, and I picked up my purse and keys and headed out.

I felt sad. He was so ready to take that huge step and I just couldn't do it. He was right. It was the best thing for us. HR would know we were together and we wouldn't have to hide things, but if Dad even got a whiff of it, I was dead to him. Okay, so I was being melodramatic, but I knew life would never be the same.

On the way to the hospital where I knew I had a change of clothes and a free shower, I stopped at the pharmacy. I got three pregnancy tests because I knew taking just one was a risk. Sometimes they were wrong, and with something this important, I couldn't afford to be wrong.

When I got to work, well ahead of the time Jack would arrive, I went to the female doctors' locker rooms. I only had a short time to get ready now, but the tests would only take a few minutes to process. So I tore all three of them open and locked myself into a shower and toilet stall. I peed on all of them and then jumped into the shower to scrub the saltiness and Jack's scent from my body.

When I was done I stepped out, dripping wet, and stood there staring at the results. All three of them had two very dark pink lines, declaring I was, in fact, pregnant. Very pregnant. Pregnant enough that all three of the tests matched and the solid lines were impossible to mistake.

I sat on the wooden bench in the stall for a moment and sighed.

This was why I was so tired, which made sense. It relieved some of my mental stress because I knew if it wasn't pregnancy, then it was likely something more serious. Then it made me feel a little nervous because while Jack was ready to take a step into a deeper relationship with me, I wasn't sure if this was something he'd want.

Then I felt happy. I smiled at myself and the situation and teared up with happy tears. Hanging out with Leah had been so wonderful. She was bright and funny and smart, and now I was going to have a baby of my own, not a borrowed child who'd never have the bond with me that a real mother-daughter relationship would have. I was going to be a mother.

"Someone in there?" I heard, and I knew I couldn't linger.

"Yeah, just a second." I had to rush to clean up, dry off, and dress, but in the back of my mind, I was less stressed than I had been in days.

I didn't know how or when to tell Jack, and I'd sit and think about that for a while, but when I did tell him, I hoped he felt as happy about this as I did. If not, I wasn't sure what to do. I'd never be able to explain it to my parents without a man to help me raise this baby.

20

JACK

"You've got to be kidding me, though. Howard, this isn't okay." I was fuming mad, so much so that I could've torn my hair out. "She can't just demand sole custody with no visitation and move out of state." I paced the expensive rug in his office and refused to be comforted.

What Dana was doing was outrageous. This was something she'd been planning for weeks or even months. I knew it. It was why she kept yelling at me for the slightest things and insisting she was going to sue. I never thought it would come to this because I didn't realize what she had going on behind the scenes. And after Leah told me she didn't like her mother's "friends", this was not going to happen. Not on my watch.

"Jack, please sit down." Howard's crinkled forehead didn't even convince me to calm down, but I did sit. This wasn't his fault, and I shouldn't be shouting in his office. "Now look, the judge has to sign off on this. What he's going to see is that you've had an agreement in place. He'll see she's living off your alimony and child support. He'll see how Dana wants to rip your child away from you to go to an environment that isn't as stable as what she has here."

"Fuck's sake," I grumbled.

"And," Howard continued calmly, "he'll see that you're an amazing father with a steady income stream. You have a solid foundation. Leah has friends here, and family. And Dana wants to take her away from all of that. All you need to do is continue to provide that stable, steady environment, and there is no way the judge will side in favor of Dana."

My chest was so tight I thought I might be having a heart attack, but I trusted Howard. He'd been my lawyer since the divorce and he'd been with me through every custody hearing. He had never steered me wrong, even when we both knew it wasn't going to go in my favor. He'd been honest then and I knew he was being honest now.

"I need some air," I told him, standing. "I'll call you tomorrow."

"Don't do anything rash, Jack. Just interact with her the same way you always would. Don't talk about this without me present!" Howard's words followed me into the hall, and I stomped all the way to my car.

If Dana thought she could swoop in here and steal my daughter away forever, she had another thing coming. I wasn't going down without a fight, but that fight was going to take everything out of me. And right now, I didn't want to be alone with my brain obsessing about it.

Before I left work, I'd told Sophia I might not want company this evening, knowing Howard had called me in for this appointment. I knew how bad they could go and figured I'd be too moody. Well, I was so moody, I knew I needed her. I sent her a quick text before I started my car to meet me at my house in fifteen minutes, then I drove like a bat out of hell. Rage didn't begin to describe what I felt.

At home, I had barely gotten to the door when Sophia's small black sedan pulled into the drive. The EV was so silent I didn't hear it until the door shut, and I turned over my shoulder to see her walking up the path. She wore a cute little skirt and a sweater, though as fall was approaching, I knew her legs were probably cold. She looked beautiful and inviting, and I wanted to devour her and forget my frustration.

"Hey," she called softly and touched my arm as I slid the key in the lock. "You feeling okay? You look upset."

I sighed and pushed the door open, and she followed me into the dark room. I didn't even bother reaching for the light switch. I shut the door and turned to pin her against the wall with a hot kiss that took her breath away.

"Jack?" she gasped when I relented and let her breathe. "What's gotten into you?"

"I need you, Soph, so bad." I felt like a wild animal that was going feral with anger and lust, and all I knew was the only time I had felt anchored in the past several months was when I was with her intimately.

"Of course," she said in compassion, but I knew she was confused.

There was no romance or tenderness, no patience or sensuality. I tore her clothes off as I groped her and smothered her further in kisses. She picked up on the heat of it and returned the gestures by clawing at me frantically and heaving for breath.

When I backed her against the kitchen island and she was pinned there naked, she braced herself on my shoulders with both arms and I lifted her by the backs of her thighs before guiding my solid-as-a-rock dick into her warmth.

"Mmm," she moaned, clenching around me as I started to pump in and out of her. She kissed me harder too, whimpering and whining as I pushed her body to the edge of pleasure.

"My God, this day," I grunted, feeling her slickness coat my length. She was it, the manacle that tethered me in place, the gravity that rooted me in hope for my future. "Fuck, you feel so good."

"Jack," she whimpered, and I pressed a thumb between her thighs on her tender spot. It drove her wild, making her body tip over into orgasm. She spasmed and jolted, and the way her pussy gripped me so tightly pushed me over the edge.

I hated to stop her enjoyment, but I had to pull out. My hand shot to my dick and I pointed it down, blowing all over the front of the cabinet door. My cum ran down the light gray paint, and I felt the tension in my body dumping out of me with the waves of endorphins.

"Whoa," she sighed, and I rubbed the end of my dick to wipe the last trace off my head, knowing I'd have a mess to wash up in a bit. Then she grabbed my wrist and brought my hand to her mouth where she sucked the few drops of my cum off my thumb. "Yummy." Sophia grinned, and I leaned into her, claiming her mouth in another heated kiss.

"So, what's got you so worked up?" she asked when I pulled my mouth away from hers and wrapped my arms around her. Still seated on my counter, she seemed distant, like something was bothering her too, but I had to get this off my chest.

"Dana's suing for sole custody. She's requested to move my daughter out of state with her. I can't let that happen, Soph. I know if the board finds out we're messing around, I'll be fired. That's the last thing I need right now. I have to continue to provide a very stable environment." Cupping her cheek, I brushed my thumb over her cheekbone and she frowned.

"So, what are you saying?" Her lip pouted out, and I knew something was bothering her. I knew what she said the other day, but that was before all of this blew up. If we were going to make this happen, it had to be done the right way. I couldn't lose my job now.

"I'm saying, I have to go to HR. It's the right thing. I'm not saying this to hurt you or pressure you. It's not an ultimatum. My daughter is just too important to me to mess this up." My heart broke knowing how much she needed my protection to keep her parents off her back, and I felt powerless.

"Alright, if it's that important to you, then I'll do it. Just please give me a few days to think about how I'll tell my parents. Because I have to tell them before we go to HR. It's the right way for me to handle it." She forced a smile, and when I opened my mouth to thank her and ask what was wrong, she pushed on my shoulders.

"Now, I was only halfway done when you so rudely stopped fucking me." She smirked and spread her legs. "Let's finish that up, shall we?"

I sank to my knees, and my lips found her pussy soaked and tender. It wasn't how I expected her to respond, but we'd have more conversations later. Of that I was certain.

21

SOPHIA

My stomach felt like I had swallowed acid. I had already thrown up three times this morning and here I was kneeling on the bathroom floor vomiting more of my lunch. Today was exceptionally bad after having an omelet with salsa on it for breakfast. I should've known better since I had already learned that anything with tomatoes made my morning sickness flare up, but I tried it hoping my body would react differently to salsa than it did to pasta sauce.

I managed to make it through morning rounds without anyone catching on that I was feeling sick, but when Jack saw me feeling queasy just before lunch, he sent me home with orders to rest and when no one was looking, a promise to stop by later. He told me I was overworked and stressed. I had no idea how to tell him I was pregnant.

After hearing how much of a mess his ex-wife was making things for him with his daughter, I knew now wasn't the right time to tell him about the baby. He didn't need another reason to fear Leah could be taken from him, though at some point, I really did have to tell him. Now I had this massive secret to juggle on my own while also trying to figure out how to inform my parents of my relationship with my boss, which would lead to my being reassigned.

If Jack wasn't in my life, I'd have just done what Andrew told me to and gone along with Mom and Dad. The pressure was too much. I knew my father only wanted what was best for me, and it was definitely in my best interests if I kept him happy, considering how much money he'd poured into my education and raising me.

Still, now that I was pregnant with Jack's baby, there was no way in hell I was moving to Maryland. I'd found happiness—despite the horrible morning sickness—that I knew I'd never find again with anyone else. Jack and I were on the same page in so many ways, and while I still feared my parents' reaction, I feared losing Jack even more. I didn't know how he'd react if I told him I couldn't go to HR. If he was irrational and too afraid of losing Leah, he might dump me.

I heard keys jingling, and then the lock on the front door clicked and I heard the hinges squeak. For a moment, I was unnerved, wondering who was walking into my apartment, but I started throwing up more and quickly forgot about it. I knew the landlord and my parents both had a key to the door, so it had to be one of them, though I didn't know why the landlord would be coming in.

When I heard my mom's soft humming I knew it was her, and I started crying. The last thing I needed was for her to see me throwing up and question it. I'd hidden it from everyone so well for the past few weeks, I thought I could keep up the charade a bit longer. But when Mom called my name softly, I started to panic, which only made the vomiting worse.

"Sophia?" she called a second time, but I was in no shape to respond. When she figured out where I was, the bathroom door swung open and she hurried to my side, holding my hair back. "Oh, Sophia... This isn't good," she said, fawning over me. Mom always did care when I was sick. She was about as nurturing as they came, doting on us and allowing us to skip school and cuddle with her. She'd even take off work to be there for us.

"Mom," I grunted, holding my hand out. She pushed a wad of toilet tissue into my palm, and I wiped my mouth and nose as she flushed the toilet.

"My heavens, that hospital needs to step up their game. Look at you so sick. I swear they have such bad records of employee sickness." She unraveled more length of toilet tissue, and I took it from her and blew my nose and sat back.

Last week's dinner had been very tense without Thomas there. He'd gone to a concert with his new fiancée. Maylin was absorbed in a new class already, talkative with Mom about how things were going, and before dinner, Andrew encouraged me to just go along with Dad's plan. Dad, however, hadn't said a word to me. We sat in ultimate silence, other than how he made wry comments about Twin Peaks in the news for a sudden surge of flu cases which the reports said had been spread by lack of sanitation.

I knew the story firsthand and tried to rebut his claims, but he was a stalwart. What really happened was an outbreak of the bird flu in a nearby elementary school and all the students whose bodies were struggling to fight it came to Twin Peaks. The newspapers would say anything to discredit medical officials and scare potential future patients. Fearmongers loved to incite fear.

"Mom, it wasn't the hospital." I blew my nose again and stood up, tossing the soiled tissue into the trash.

"Yes, well, dear, the news said—"

"Mom, can we drop it?" I helped her to her feet while she scowled at me. She and Dad would say anything they could to sway my opinion of Twin Peaks Memorial and my coworkers. They wanted me to look down on it as a valid means of education, even if it made me look down on myself at the same time.

"I just think you wouldn't be sick if they took better precautions. Now come lie down on the couch." I followed her into the living room, finally feeling a little better. There was so much on my mind lately that it was hard to think about cleaning my apartment. Plus, I'd spent so much time at Jack's place, I had barely come home. This was more of a pitstop than a home now.

"Mom, why are you here?" As I flopped onto the clothes-covered sofa, I noticed the stack of boxes she'd carried in and I knew it meant one thing. I'd have come home from work with a lot of my apartment packed up as if I were ready to move. Mom picked up one of the boxes and folded it open, then weaved the bottom flaps together so it was shut. She started shoving my couch throw pillows into it.

"I'm helping you get packed up, Sophia." She said it so matter-of-factly that it left no room for me to have an opinion or protest, but I definitely had opinions. "We just have to pick the right apartment. Your father has all the leases ready to go. There are so many good choices."

As she prattled about apartment choices, location within the city and distance to work, I grew angrier and angrier. And I was glad I had already thrown up all my stomach contents or I'd have tossed my cookies again right there.

"And the last option is across from the lake, and you won't believe the—"

"Enough!" I'd never shouted at my mother, never raised my voice in her presence or Dad's. I was taught to be more respectful and quiet, but I'd had enough. "I'm not moving." I stood up and shook my head, shoving my hands into my scrubs pocket. "I'm staying at Twin Peaks."

"Dear, you don't mean that. Your father has gone to all the trouble of—"

"I said no, Mom." I was standing my ground and I wasn't going to back down this time. Mom seemed to get the point and her shoulders fell. "I want to make it on my own, Mom. I want to do things for myself, not because Dad opened doors for me or sought favors. I just want you to believe in me." The fatigue I'd been dealing with started to get to me and I felt lightheaded. I sat down on the couch, and she joined me.

"Sophia, you're making your own life too hard. We don't want you to have to struggle the way we did." She took my hand and squeezed it, and I felt the urge to pull it away in haste, but I didn't.

"The struggle is part of what made you as determined as you are. I think I deserve to have that choice for myself." My bottom lip quivered and I wanted to cry, but I blinked back the tears. Mom didn't need to see me emotional. She needed to see me being bold and independent.

"Oh, your father's not going to like this at all." Her head hung, but she sighed. "I'll go. I'm sorry. Do you want me to bring you anything?"

It was sweet that she still cared and wanted to take care of me. "No, Mom. I just want to rest." What I really wanted was for her to get out of my place before Jack came by because I didn't need that conflict too. I already had too much weight on my shoulders.

"Alright. I'll call to check on you before bed." Mom stood and kissed my forehead then left my house, but she left the boxes with me.

The days of my parents controlling my decisions were over. I had to stand my ground. I was going to have Jack's baby, and I couldn't just up and leave town and not tell him. Not if I ever wanted him to look at me again.

22

JACK

It was a labor-intensive week again. Sophia and I were both exhausted and with having Leah over, we decided tonight wasn't a good night for her to sleep over. Though, I had come to that decision reluctantly. I knew how difficult it would be to shut off and fall asleep without her next to me. She'd been spending so much time at my house up until a few days ago when she got sick at work that she had begun leaving a change of clothes here and put a spare toothbrush in my bathroom.

When I approached her about declaring the relationship, she promised me that she would discuss it with her parents first, then we could do it together. I had to respect that. I knew this declaration would mean a switch in jobs for her, and while the fallout of the relationship getting out to Dana would potentially make my personal dynamic dicier and potentially give her lawyer fuel for discrediting my ability to parent, it didn't feel like it would affect me as quickly as the sudden ninety-degree turn in her career would affect her.

I had to bide my time and do things by the book. I tried to rationalize that if Dana found out, it wouldn't be the worst thing. She was dating too, and while Sophia was actually a very upstanding member of society whom Leah loved, the men Dana was dating were clearly not quite on the same level. If Dana tried to make it sound like I was putting bad influences around our daughter, I could swing the sword both ways.

My qualm was if the board found out about Sophia and me and what they'd say. It likely would come down to however they interpreted things, which would mean one or both of us would be punished and potentially fired. If that happened, Dana would have the gasoline she needed to torch my custody stance. I couldn't let that happen.

The car rolled to a stop in front of Dana's house and I noticed the lights were off, all except the single light in the kitchen. As I walked toward the house, I saw her seated at the kitchen table with a cigarette in hand, smoking. I didn't know when she'd picked up the nasty habit, but I wasn't thrilled with the fact that she was doing it in a home where Leah lived while she was actively home.

I wanted to tell her how much that angered me, but I had to trust Howard's advice. I had to keep my mouth shut and keep a dependable and stable environment for Leah. If I wanted to complain about this, I had to bring it up with the judge. This might change things in his eyes. Maybe not, but picking a fight with Dana definitely wouldn't help things.

I knocked on the door and heard Dana shout Leah's name. Then the door swung open and she stood there with a burning cigarette in hand looking tired and haggard with one arm over her stomach and her elbow planted on her wrist. Smoke rose upward from the lit cigarette and she scowled at me.

"So you finally decide to start showing up on time when you're scheduled? I thought I had a few hours left." The sardonic reply made me irritated, but I plastered a fake smile on my face.

"Is Leah ready? I can wait in the car if she's not." I listened intently but only heard the sound of the TV blaring in the other room.

"She's not coming tonight," Dana said, and it confused me. It was my night to have my daughter, and Dana had just called her down.

"Why not?" I asked, suddenly feeling defensive. I knew my forehead was displaying the signals, a deep, furrowed brow, stormy eyes.

But I tried to keep my tone light. Arguing would not serve my purpose.

"Why not? Because you'll have that hoe Sophia over again." My heart clenched at the comment, and she just kept talking. "Yeah, you thought you were sneaky, bringing women into your house with Leah around. I know you're fucking her while our kid is in the house, and I don't even know what sort of person she is."

"I told you, Mommy. She's a doctor like Daddy." Leah's chipper voice broke through the tension between me and my ex-wife, and I swallowed my rage like medicine. I would not break down and argue with Dana in front of Lean.

"Hey, baby, go run and climb in Daddy's car." I gestured, but Dana put her hand in front of Leah's chest and stopped her.

"I told you, she's not coming." Dana held Leah back, but my little girl was so good and respectful, she didn't argue. She just stood there with a pleading expression and I decided I had to get firm or I'd lose my weekend. Then Dana would tell the court I stopped taking her when it was my turn.

"Dana, let me remind you that you are bringing men into this house whom I have never met." It was a struggle to keep my even keel, but I was managing. I just kept glancing at Leah, and it reminded me what I was fighting for. At this point, I wasn't fighting Dana. I was fighting my own anger. "I could say the same about you. Now, it's my weekend, and I have the custody agreement saved to my phone in a file. Unless you want me to call the police to come settle this, you'll let Leah leave with me."

"Who is she?" Dana spat, and I had zero intention of answering that question. It'd been years since we split and she had no right to ask that of me. I never questioned the people she was friends with or the men she dated. Though, Dana and I still hung in the same circles. We had friends who wouldn't invite us both to events for fear of there being drama. I could be civil, but Dana never would.

"It's none of your business," I told her, reaching my hand to Leah. She scurried to my side and held my hand, and I told Dana, "Listen, I'm not supposed to talk to you about this. Howard warned me to say nothing, but I thought I'd let you know. I'm considering suing you back for sole custody. You can't just take Leah and move to another state. I'm not just going to take it lying down."

Dana spat at my feet, with no regard for what she was teaching Leah. I knew she didn't care one bit about our daughter. She only wanted to hurt me. I had, in her mind, destroyed something inside her that she'd never get back, and this was her punishment. My heart broke for the relationship Leah would never have with her mother.

"Come on, Leah," I said, and I turned and walked us to the car.

We were halfway home before Leah spoke up, and when she did, it made me feel sad. "I'm sorry, Daddy. I didn't mean to make Mommy mad at you."

I looked at her reflection in my rearview mirror and sighed. "It's not your fault, baby. Mommy is just sad and angry. Okay?"

Above all, the last thing I'd ever want to do was damage the relationship Leah had with her mother. Someday, she'd grow up and realize it for herself, but I wanted no part of being the one who broke her.

"But she was so mad at you and Sophia. I like Sophia." Leah wistfully stared out the window, and I thought I saw her crying, but I heard no sniffling.

"You do, huh? Well, Sophia has been working too hard this week and she feels a little tired and sick, so she won't be here this weekend. But maybe next time you come by."

Leah got quiet for a while, and it dawned on me that because Dana cared so little for her, she probably hadn't even asked her opinion about moving. What a horrible thing to do to a child whose parents are no longer together and live in different homes. It would feel like ripping her heart out.

"Did Mommy ask you about having a new house? Going to a new school?" I asked, gauging what she knew.

Leah's eyes seemed frightened and she shook her head. "No. I don't want a new school. I like my friends."

I sighed hard again. Dana planned to do all of this without even discussing it with Leah. That angered me more than just the idea of her doing this at all.

"Well, if you had to live with Mommy and her new boyfriend or me at my house, what would you choose?" I pulled up to a red light and stopped, and it gave me a chance to turn over my shoulder and watch her facial expression shift.

"Can Sophia live with us too? Because if she does, then I want to live with you." Her face lit up like the Fourth of July, and I chuckled.

"Well, we'd have to ask Sophia that, but let's just say I have a good feeling she'd want to. She likes you more than she likes me."

Leah clapped and laughed, and for the rest of the ride we talked only about Sophia, the light in my child's life. I could've said I was jealous of her, but in reality, I was seeing my little girl happier than she'd been in years, and it was all because of the woman I was falling head over heels in love with.

Now to figure out how to make a judge, the board of trustees, and my ex-wife see that Leah's being with me and Sophia was the best thing for her. All in a way that got neither of us fired.

23

SOPHIA

When I knocked on Jack's door Friday night, I'd come ready to tell him about the baby. I'd been wrestling with it all week long, ever since Mom showed up at my apartment. I realized I couldn't very well tell my parents about me and Jack and the potential for my job being totally screwed up if I didn't first tell Jack about the baby. If he had an adverse reaction to it, it might change everything, leaving me with no job and no partner.

Jack opened and seemed grouchy. He let me in, but it was late, and I felt like I had interrupted something. He'd sent me home from work ordering me to rest and hydrate. The nausea and fatigue I'd been suffering were entirely from my pregnancy, which I had stopped trying to hide. Jack blamed it on stress and being overworked and never for a second mentioned any suspicions about it being a pregnancy.

"I thought we agreed you'd stay home and rest," he grumbled, and I got the feeling I wasn't wanted there until Leah burst into the room and cheered. She ran straight toward me and wrapped her arms around my waist.

I hugged her back, and my internal resolve to give Jack the news was waning. "Hey, Leah, I didn't know you were here this weekend." I glanced up at Jack, who waved a dismissive hand and shut the door.

"Daddy said you were sick. Are you feeling better?" she asked, and then she let me go.

I winced and smiled at her. This was going to be harder than I thought. The lies were out there, and I had to fix it right away, but with Jack's mood and the fact that he had Leah over, I wasn't sure tonight was still a good night.

"Go finish your dinner," he grumbled at Leah, who blew me a kiss and ran off.

I turned to him and frowned. "Are you okay, bud?" I reached for him, but he just took my hand and led me to the kitchen where Leah sat at the table eating.

"Dana and I had it out earlier. We can talk later." Jack bustled around the kitchen cleaning up, so I helped him. It was late for dinner, which meant he'd been stressed or something. Leah was normally in bed by now, and Jack was usually relaxing and ready to lie down soon. I had hoped to catch him before sleep, and while I did do just that, I felt bad for interrupting his time with Leah.

"Alright, Leah. Go brush your teeth and I'll be there to tuck you in." Jack picked up her empty plate and juice cup, and Leah waved at me.

"I'm going to brush my teeth. Sophia, you can tuck me in too if you want." What I didn't expect was when Jack walked past me, Leah raced over and wrapped her arms around both of us at once. "This is my family, and I want to live with this family." Her cheery smile made my emotions get all tangled up.

"Leah, go on," Jack growled, and I didn't know if it was something she'd said or if she'd just been naughty earlier in the evening and this was hangover from that.

Leah raced off as happy as can be, and I took the plate from Jack's hand and walked to the sink. "What's going on?" I asked again. It really wasn't the best night to tell him I was going to have his baby, but now that I was here and I noticed how upset he was, I couldn't leave him like this.

"Just..." He raked a hand through his hair. "Just go wait in my room?" His eyes were full of pain, not anger. I'd always heard that anger was a secondary emotion, and this just proved it. His grumpiness was because he was worried about something. I wondered if he'd put two and two together and realized I was keeping a secret.

"Of course," I told him as he walked out.

I rinsed the plates and loaded them into the dishwasher, then threw out the takeout containers. When I was done wiping the table down, I went to his bed and sat down. I could hear him reading Leah a book, and I heard her asking for me too, but he didn't call me in. I felt a little sad about that, but I had no idea what had happened to upset him. For all I knew, it was a punishment for her poor behavior.

But while I sat there eavesdropping, I also started to wonder if maybe Jack was just realizing that I was a bad idea. Maybe his little girl was getting too attached to me and he wasn't fond of that. If maybe having a happy little family didn't play into his plans for his life, and if maybe my being reluctant to go to HR about us had been the final straw.

I sat there wringing my hands waiting for him, and when he came in and lay down on the bed with a sour expression, I was afraid to talk. He rubbed his face and when he rested his hands on his chest, his eyes were shut. I waited, and I was glad I did. I'd have asked a dumb question about my worth to him or something, when none of this was about me—well, sort of.

"Dana knows about you."

"What?" I asked. At first, I didn't remember that his ex-wife's name was Dana, but he quickly reminded me.

"Yeah, Leah's been telling her how amazing you are." His eyes popped open and he rolled to his side. "She's furious."

I narrowed my eyes in confusion and shrugged a shoulder. "So let her be mad?" I didn't understand why this was a big deal.

"She and I have mutual friends. If she starts asking around, someone is going to start snooping too. These are people I still work with, Sophia." He sighed hard, and I felt how frustrated he was. "If she asks them, and they know your first name is Sophia, it's only a matter of time before someone reports us to HR, someone who is loyal to Dana and not me."

"That's horrible." I felt so sad and I didn't know how to say anything that would make a difference. "She's just out to hurt you."

"It's been that way since she decided she wanted out. The other men, the lies, keeping Leah from me." Jack pulled his pillow under his head and laid it down.

I wanted to make him feel better, but telling him there was yet another complication to this messy situation wasn't going to help. Tonight wasn't the night after all, and in fact, I was probably going to have to tell my parents everything before I let Jack know this secret.

"What can I do?" I asked, and I knew there was really nothing, but he reached for me.

"Stay with me." The way he pulled me toward himself until I was lying down, struggling to get my feet out from under me, was all the explanation I needed. I kicked my shoes off and pushed them off the bed and let him capture my lips in a kiss.

"Jack," I whispered, but he was too eager, too intent on sating his body with mine. I didn't mind, and in fact, I wanted him too. I just wished this were a celebration of our love and the fact that we were having a baby.

"Don't worry, I have a condom," he growled, and he rolled on top of me.

Jack's hands were all over me, groping and tearing my clothes off. I returned in kind with the same level of passion. At first I was only thinking of him, but the nastier he got, the hornier I got. Until we were both naked, panting, and clawing at each other.

Jack turned me over, face down on the bed, and hoisted my hips into the air. His teeth raked across my backside as his hands spread me apart, and then his stubble scraped my tender skin, coating his face in moisture. His fingers found my opening, and he roughly pushed two inside me, stretching me while his thumb rubbed at my clit.

"Tell me you want this," he growled in my ear, but I could barely think straight enough to form a complete sentence, let alone get the words past my lips.

"I–I want it," I managed to gasp out, but it was enough for him. He withdrew his fingers, and in the place of his fingers came the head of his cock. I wasn't expecting it, and it made me suck in a breath and hiss as he filled me. He used his thumb to smear my own moisture on my ass, then pumped a few more times.

"God, I want this," Jack growled, pushing a thumb into the tight, hot ring of muscles, and I didn't care what he did to me as long as he finished me.

"Yes," I whimpered, and I backed toward him, sinking his thumb further into my body.

He seemed to respond with pleasure. His other thumb sank into my pussy, drenching it in my juices, and then pushed into my ass with the other. I whimpered and clenched, and I found my clit and rubbed. I was so close if he didn't just put it in me now, I was going to come so hard and spasm and he'd never get it in.

"You ready?" he asked, and I whimpered my acknowledgment.

With a deep breath, he plunged into me, and I screamed. It hurt, but it also felt so good, the stretching and being full of him. He pumped in and out of me, thrusting hard and fast. His hands gripped my hips, squeezing the flesh in his fists as he slammed into me roughly. I bit my lip trying to keep quiet.

"Let it go, baby, come for me," he groaned in my ear, and with those words, I lost control.

The room around us vanished as wave after wave washed over me. He bottomed out inside me, growling like an animal as his body consumed mine. I convulsed and spasmed, happy the pillow was there to bite down on. I thought of Leah briefly and not wanting to wake her. Jack seemed to have no thought other than release, which he found shortly after my orgasm waned.

I felt him flood me, and I closed my eyes as his thrusts slowed, gritting my teeth against the friction of being penetrated almost completely dry.

When he pulled out, it was relief and pleasure all at once. I collapsed and he curled around me, though he kept his hands to himself. I lay there heaving for a moment while he lay behind me catching his breath. When the heaviness of post-orgasmic endorphins was beginning to make me drowsy, he pulled away.

I heard the faucet in the bathroom running and rolled out of bed. I knew the best chance he had for keeping his job, and thus keeping Leah, was for us to just go to HR. I knew how it would look to my parents, and I knew no matter how we told them or how we prepared them for the news, Dad would be upset. Mom would freak out but later, she'd be sympathetic, but the most important part was that they'd get over it eventually.

I couldn't bear to put the anxiety on Jack's shoulders.

"Hey," I said softly, coming up behind him while he washed his hands. He was stiff, still tense, but his gaze caught my reflection in the mirror.

"I'm, uh... I'm sorry if I was too rough."

"No, not at all." I kissed the back of his shoulder. I loved that we could be naked together and unashamed. "Baby, if you need to go to HR right now to make this thing legit, then count me in."

I said the words knowing full well the weight of the consequences it would be for me, but some things were more important than my own mental peace.

"You mean that?" he asked, turning around to look me in the eye. He reached past me to the towel rack and grabbed the towel to dry his hands.

"I mean it. Let's do it Monday." I nodded resolutely even as my stomach started to churn again. I must've looked a little green because Jack grimaced.

"Alright, we'll go Monday. But for now, you go lie down. I can tell you're working too hard."

He shooed me out of the bathroom and I obeyed his gesture. Now if I could just get my stomach to obey my will to not throw up, I'd be getting somewhere.

I hoped the nuclear fallout after this announcement wasn't too

SILVER FOX'S INTERN DILEMMA

bad, or else Jack might have a lot more than he bargained for. I might actually have to move in with him just to survive.

24

JACK

I stood across the surgical table from Sophia with my gloved hands coated in blood. She was holding the retractor as I made the necessary cuts to resect a tumor on a patient's esophagus. She seemed distant and a bit slower than normal, which only confirmed to me that our long hours and extra time spent studying were getting to her. I'd told her to sit this one out, but she insisted that she was fine.

I watched carefully what I was doing, but her posture slumped and she looked tired.

"You okay, Dr. Chen?" I asked, and she nodded.

"Fine, Dr. Thornton." The short, one-word answers were frustrating to me. I'd asked her several times during this surgery alone, and now that we were almost finished, she seemed very much not fine at all.

"Nurse, please take Dr. Chen's spot and let her go sit down." I knew showing my concern for her was risky. The only reason to do this was because I felt she was failing professionally or because I was concerned with her performance. Neither were true. I was really just concerned with her as a friend, or more than a friend. We hadn't really discussed it, but I was ready to tell this woman I loved her in every sense of the word, and the minute that HR meeting was over, I intended to tell her.

"Dr. Thornton, I'm fine," Sophia protested, and she squared her shoulders, but I could see clearly that something was wrong.

The nurse looked up at me as I laid the clamp with the resected tumor on the specimen tray and reached for the surgical needle. She looked worried, and I scowled but nodded to her to stay put for the moment. Sophia was being stubborn, which was typically a good trait for a doctor to have when they knew they were right, but in this instance, I felt something was off about her.

"Keep the retractor open. I have to get these sutures in now." I focused again on the task, taking the needle to the incision site. I put in seven stitches there and then allowed Sophia to remove the chest retractor and relax for a second. As I began stitching the exterior incision, however, she pressed the back of her wrist to her forehead. Her hands had blood on them, but I could see her trying to avoid getting it on herself.

I looked up at her, and the expression in her eyes was hazy, confused, maybe. Then she blinked.

"I don't feel so good," Sophia mumbled, and I barely had time to react.

"Nurse!" I shouted, but Sophia was already on her way down. She hit the floor like a ton of bricks and instruments clattered everywhere. My heart leapt into my throat at the sight, but I couldn't very well rush around and touch her. I had a patient with an open chest cavity who needed to be stitched up.

"Get a gurney," I barked and tore my eyes away from Sophia. I had to focus. This was no time to let my emotions get out of control. This was the exact reason the hospital non-frat policy existed.

If I let my feelings for her or my concern about her change the way I treated this patient, I would only prove to HR that I was unable to work with someone I had feelings for. I was shaking, my shoulders tense, but I stared down at the open chest cavity in front of me and took a deep breath.

"Get Dr. Briggs in here now. Get her out of here. Take her to emergency."

If I so much as stuck a needle into this man, I was going to mess up, so I waited. It took Dr. Briggs only five minutes to rush in, and when he stood opposite me, I handed him the needle and said, "I need you to do this."

"Something wrong?" he asked, but he took the needle without complaint.

I stayed there. He was only a resident, and he wasn't allowed to perform surgery by himself, but he was already doing simple ones, and sutures to close an incision were something he had mastered.

"I just watched Dr. Chen collapse and I'm feeling a bit shaken. I want to do what I know is best for the patient." My firm statement left no room for him to question me, though I knew later on there would be lots of questions. He was the first one, after all, who had seen the shift between us.

It was torture waiting for him to finish up. I said nothing to him as I scrubbed out, and then I raced to the emergency room. It was no more than twenty minutes, but by the time I got to Sophia's side, she was sitting up with a glass of water, sipping it carefully. Her scrubs had a bit of blood, but I knew it belonged to the patient. And she looked so tired and pale, I thought for sure that something horrible was wrong. What had appeared to be exhaustion from work could be anything from a brain disorder to a heart condition.

"Jack, I'm so sorry," she said, setting the cup to the side. The nurse who was checking her vitals nodded at me and rushed out as soon as she heard my first name and not my title. I knew the cat was out of the bag now, or if it wasn't, it would be soon. I'd have no choice but to go to HR now.

"Soph, I was so worried." Without thinking, and definitely without her permission, I reached for the tablet on the counter. Sophia's chart was on there, and I had to know what tests they were ordering. Of course, the typical round would be a complete blood count and metabolic panel, but with a woman, they'd also potentially run hormone panels too. My mind raced with the possibilities. I was a surgeon, not a diagnostician, but I knew enough.

"Jack, please."

She reached for me, but my eyes were already poring over the tablet screen. She sounded fearful, though, not upset. Whatever it was, I could help her. I had to know I couldn't lose her. Not now, not when we were so close to having what I knew we both wanted.

"Please, Jack." Sophia was crying now, and I didn't know why.

They had ordered the exact tests I suspected, with the exception of one. No pregnancy test. But why?

I raised my eyebrows and then looked up at her. "They are testing for everything but pregnancy... That's not right. I need to make them add that in. If you're—" My brain caught up with my words as I spoke and my hands felt heavy. I let them fall to my sides and almost dropped the tablet. The only reason they'd skip that test was if she told them she was on her period—or that she was already pregnant.

"Soph?" I said, taking the few steps to her bedside. I sat down, and she nodded, then smiled. Then she swiped at her tears and covered her mouth, but though she seemed happy and almost on the verge of laughing, her forehead was scrunched up in fear.

"You're..." I couldn't say it. I didn't want to jinx this. I searched her face with my gaze, and she nodded again.

"Yes, I am." When she blinked, large crocodile tears streamed down her cheeks and she reached for my hand. "But they called my parents already. They'll be here any second, and I don't want them to know yet."

"You're having my baby?" I asked again, still not believing it. No wonder she'd been so tired and sick. I was such a fool. That first time we had sex... I messed that up, and now...

Sophia laughed and cried and wiped her tears away again and nodded, and a sudden burst of glee flooded me. I gripped both sides of her face and leaned in and kissed her, letting the tablet slip from my lap onto the floor. It clattered there while I stole the most passionate kiss from her I'd ever felt. None of this was supposed to happen, but not a single bit of it felt out of place.

"My God, woman, I love you." I kissed her again as she gripped my biceps and tried to push me off her, and we both chuckled.

"Dr. Thornton?" The same nurse stood in the doorway, and I pulled away, not even ashamed at all anymore. "Dr. Chen's parents are here."

"Go," she said, swatting me away, and I smiled at her.

"Guess I'm going to HR," I told her with my eyebrows high, and she smiled and wiped her tears again.

"Send them in," Sophia said, and for a moment I thought to stay with her and help her give her parents the news, but she raised her eyebrows insistently. It appeared she wasn't quite ready for that much.

So I wandered out of her room with my head reeling, both in shock and in happiness. My God, this was going to mess things up in such a beautiful way. I had to call Howard. Whatever happened with Leah and Dana, I couldn't let a surprise like this affect it. Life just got a whole lot more complicated.

25

SOPHIA

Jack rushed out and Mom and Dad walked in moments later. I didn't even have time to think about Jack's reaction or what it meant for us. He seemed happy, though, not angry or anxious about it like I feared he may be. With everything going on with his custody hearing and how his ex-wife was trying to steal his little girl away, I figured he'd have had a stronger reaction, but I was wrong. And maybe this wasn't a horrible thing after all.

"Oh, baby," Mom said, rushing to my side. She sat on the edge of the bed where Jack had just been, and Dad followed her in. He stood on the other side of the bed. The nurse picked up the tablet Jack had dropped and glanced at me.

"I'll leave you alone to visit for now. When that IV bag is done, we can get you out of here, but you need to go home and rest. I'll make sure Dr. Hinkler is okay with that. Probably put you on some multivitamins too."

I was so glad the nurse used the word multivitamin and not prenatal. I made it clear to everyone the minute I came to and found myself in this bed that they were to keep their mouths shut. Jack finding out was inevitable, but I had hoped to tell him a bit differently. Mom and Dad, however, were not going to find out today or anytime soon.

137

I still had to figure out how to tell them about Jack and about the possibility of a change in my residency because of dating him. If I told them I was pregnant, they'd think he had complete disregard for me and my future. But the truth was that it was completely mutual, what happened, and it wasn't supposed to happen this way.

"You passed out during surgery?" Dad asked sternly, and I felt ashamed. I knew I'd been feeling weak, but I didn't think it was that bad. I figured a bit of caffeine would help pick me up once the surgery was over. I didn't know I was so anemic.

"Yeah, I've been sick and—"

"It's true," Mom told him. "I was at her house the other day and she was very ill." Mom turned to me and frowned. "I told you to rest. Now you just went and made yourself sicker. It's good they prescribed the vitamins. Are you even eating? You look pale."

Mom doted on me, checking my temperature with the back of her hand on my forehead and clicked her tongue. My insides were all tangled up. If I just told them I was really pregnant and anemic, I wouldn't feel the guilt of lying, but there were so many complications. I couldn't just blurt it out. Besides, I didn't think I could handle the emotional toll it would take on my heart right now to see my father's disappointment.

"I'm fine," I said, swatting her hand away. "I'm under a lot of stress." I bit my lower lip and thought of how she walked in on me throwing up. My mom was a very smart woman. Too many more instances like this and she'd figure it out.

"What is so stressful? If you think residency is stressful, you might want to rethink a surgical career path." Dad was so practical, so no-nonsense. I found it hard to relate with him at times. He was black and white. If I couldn't live under the high-stakes pressure of emergency surgeries, I'd never amount to anything and I might as well go for a lesser career goal. I hated that mentality—that I couldn't stretch myself or grow.

"If you didn't keep pushing me to do better, be better, go farther..." I felt my bottom lip quiver as his eyebrows rose. I could see the frustration in his eyes, that he wanted to snap at me. But I was here in a hospital bed and Mom was seated next to me holding my hand. He let me continue without correcting me.

"Mom shows up at my apartment to pack my things without asking me. You line up jobs for me that I don't want. If your parents did that for you, you'd never have come to this country. You insisted it was what was best for you, but you don't always know what's best for other people." I was huffing, ready to cry, and Dad's forehead relaxed and then he looked sad.

"You really don't want to go to Baltimore?" For the first time in my life, my father was asking me what I wanted. I didn't even know how to respond.

I shrugged my shoulders and blinked back tears. "I want to stay here. I've been saying how much I like being closer to you and Mama. Baba, it's not that I don't trust you or that I don't see how prestigious Johns Hopkins is. I do. But I need my family close to me. And I want to do things on my own, make my own choices, even if life is more difficult that way."

This conversation had been a long time coming. I was just glad they were actually listening to me. All it took was me collapsing at work and winding up in a bed in the ER for them to notice, but at least it wasn't something more serious. It was a run-of-the-mill case of anemia. A lot of pregnant women developed it, and it was easily treatable with a healthier diet and vitamins.

I yawned and blinked slowly and glanced up at the IV bag. I had at least another hour of this, but I was so drained. "I think I need to rest. Is that okay?" I asked, and Mom nodded.

"Of course, *qiān jīn*," Dad said softly. "You rest." He tapped the arm rail of the bed and sighed. "If you feel so strongly and it's causing you so much stress that you collapse at work, perhaps you're right. Being closer to your family is the best for you..." He looked thoughtful, then added, "You will stay with us while you fully recover, and your Mama and I will make sure you're eating properly."

He left very little room for argument in that statement, and I knew I wasn't getting out of it. Even at twenty-eight, I would be forced to stay with my parents for a few days while this blew over. But I conceded with a small frown and a nod. I had won the greater battle, so it was okay to wave the white flag now.

"Thank you, Baba," I told him, and he kissed my forehead before they walked out.

If I had to stay with them for a few days to appease his need to control things, it was about as good of a trade off as anything else. I lay my head back on the pillow and shut my eyes.

My secret was out. Partially. Jack knew, and while his opinion was what mattered most, I knew it was just the beginning of the drama. They say you can only eat an elephant one bite at a time, and I felt like this monster of a revelation was one I had to spoon feed my parents. I'd taken the first step by putting my foot down, and now I was definitely staying in Denver. The next step was working through whatever challenging emotions Jack had regarding a baby and making our announcement to HR.

I hadn't even gotten to the part of Jack telling his daughter, or the lawyer, or even his ex-wife. I was the one who needed to pace myself now. Because if Jack wasn't as thrilled as I was about having this baby, things could go sideways very quickly. And now, with my parents hovering, I knew I wouldn't get the opportunity to speak to Jack for a while. I just prayed his initial response of happiness wasn't faked simply because I was lying in a hospital bed.

26

JACK

I didn't have to ask which set of concerned people were Sophia's parents. She looked exactly like her mother and I spotted them approaching the door as I walked out. Her father, a middle-aged man with a balding head, round face, and a wisp of a combover, looked very stern. He was exactly what I expected based on Sophia's accounts of how she'd been raised. I nodded at them respectfully and passed by, on my way to the doctors' lounge.

My heart felt so full yet so conflicted at the same time. My chest cavity felt like it was physically swelling with all the emotion. I knew as a physician that it was the release of my fight or flight hormones, surging through me with the shock. It started in the operating room and had continued ever since. For a brief moment when I saw that Sophia was okay, I felt better, but when she told me the news, I felt a bit dizzy myself from the adrenaline rush.

So I was going to be a father again. The shock of it was so much, I had to sit down. I found a chair in the corner of the lounge and crumpled my scrub cap in my hands as I leaned my head against the wall and shut my eyes. It made total sense now why Sophia had been dragging her feet about going to HR. It wasn't just about her parents and their opinion about her internship. Now she had a secret from them that would cause a lot more than work stress.

"Dr. Thornton, are you okay?" I heard Dr. Briggs's voice and opened my eyes. He'd come up to the lounge after scrubbing out, though he'd probably gone to my office first for the debrief. I hadn't even thought about it. The moment I was scrubbed, I ran straight to emergency. I sat a bit straighter and rubbed my face.

"Yeah, uh... Thanks for stepping in last-minute." I felt grateful for him but also a bit shaken and embarrassed. He'd had to jump in at the last minute, though his training had prepared him for it.

"No problem." He pulled up a chair and sat down, taking off his own scrub cap. "I guess you went to the ER to see Dr. Chen?"

"Yeah, she's alright. Anemic... But I was worried." I hoped my fondness for her wasn't too obvious, but at this point, it was only a matter of time until everyone knew, anyway. I had to go to HR, but after that announcement, I felt like I should go to her first. We had a lot to discuss.

How would Leah take this? What would the lawyer think? Would Dana freak out more and get even more hostile? Hell, what did I even think about this? I was thinking about how a new baby would affect current circumstances without even reflecting on what it meant for me. I was officially dedicating the next twenty years of my life to raising another child. I'd be almost sixty by the time this was over, but something inside me sparked with joy when I thought about it.

"You okay?" Dr. Briggs asked, and I shrugged a shoulder. We'd worked together long enough that he knew me well enough to know something was going on. I just couldn't come out and tell him what it actually was until I had that fateful conversation with HR. There were enough hints now for him to begin drawing his own conclusions, though without proof, no one could point a finger.

"I'm alright. I'm just exhausted. The workload is taking a toll on me too." I forced a weak smile, and he nodded.

Dr. Briggs knocked twice on the table situated between us and then stood. "What I know is if someone I cared about was in the ER, I wouldn't be worrying about work." He gave me a pointed look, and I tried my hardest not to respond, but I could tell he was reading me like a book. "I'll see you tomorrow. Hopefully, Dr. Chen is feeling better soon."

"Have a good night," I told him and watched him walk out.

Sophia and I had been having fun. We'd snuck around, had wild sex, gotten to know each other, and at times, I'd felt a deeper connection with her than I had anyone else in my entire life. When the heat got turned up with the custody case, I knew it was time to take things more seriously and I wanted to. I wanted to declare our relationship and go to HR—do things the right way. I still wanted that, but now there was an added element of upheaval.

Sophia wasn't anywhere close to having a stable career. She had at least four and a half years of residency training left. That was assuming her parents let her stay here in Denver. I couldn't imagine her being gone, but I had to think about what was best for her now and the baby. If for some stupid reason things between us fell apart or didn't work out, she'd be a single mother. She was at the precipice of greatness in her career, and maybe that internship at Johns Hopkins really was what she should do.

But I'd never be able to tell her that. It would mean hurting her, to agree with her father... It would be pushing her away, sending her across the country where we had to resort to phone calls and emails. I didn't want her that far from me, but it wasn't like we were ready to be married. I'd made that choice with Dana and it screwed me up. We got married so quickly, and it fell apart even faster.

I wanted Sophia, but I wanted to do things the right way. And against all odds, I wanted that baby too. I'd be a fool to make any sort of decision that would hurt her or our child. I just didn't know what the right choice was, and I didn't know how to make it.

My thoughts were interrupted when I got called to check on a post-op patient, and by the time I got down to the ER to see Sophia again, she'd been discharged. The nurse told me she left with her parents and hadn't given any notes or anything. As her boss, I had a good reason for following up, but as her lover, I was more interested in just knowing she was okay.

I nodded off in the on-call room, but I left my phone on just in case she called. Life just got a lot more complicated, as if I needed it. But I was seeing a ray of hope on the horizon. Sophia and I would work this out. I knew we would. I just wondered what hell we'd be walking through to get to the other side.

27

SOPHIA

I lay curled in a ball on the guest bed in my parents' house stuck in my head. When Jack never came back to the ER yesterday to check on me, I had no choice but to go with my parents. I agreed to Dad's orders with only a bit of frustration, but after he had doubled back and given me his blessing to stay here in Denver, I felt I owed him that much. But it left me feeling uneasy and worried.

Jack just found out he was going to be a father all over again, something I wasn't sure he was ready for. And while his reaction to the news seemed to be positive at first, I knew it had the potential to really mess things up. And on top of all of that, when I left the hospital, I hadn't brought my phone with me. It was locked in my locker with my street clothes where I left it so Jack had no way to contact me, and I wasn't about to use my parents' phone to call him.

I sighed and turned over, staring up at the ceiling in the dark room. Maylin would be home soon for her visit with the family this weekend. She'd hear how I passed out at work and wonder what was going on with me. I'd hidden the prenatals, so that wasn't going to be an issue. The problem would be lying to her and convincing her that I was just tired and exhausted, especially given how emotional I'd been. She'd see right through it.

She and I told each other everything, really, and I felt so full of stress and worry about everything that I didn't know what to do. I wanted someone to talk to. Someone who knew my parents well enough to know how they'd respond to me when I confessed that Id' slept with my boss, gotten pregnant, tanked my entire career, put his custody of his own daughter in jeopardy, and all of this while I defied my own parents. If anyone would sympathize with me, it was Maylin.

I dozed off somewhere in late afternoon, and when I woke up it was to the sound of the front door shutting loudly. Mom and Dad greeted my sister, and then I heard hushed talking. They thought I was resting and probably didn't realize that I could tell they were talking about me. My suspicions were confirmed when someone knocked on the door and it started to open. For a second I thought it was Mom, so I pretended to be sleeping. But Maylin whispered my name and I opened my eyes.

She slipped into the room and turned on the light, and I scooted over in bed for her to join me. Her expression was one of sympathy and concern, but I knew when she heard what a mess I'd made of my life, she'd be as nervous as I was. Choosing my own career path was one thing. A baby was next-level trouble.

"Hey, Mom said you passed out at work?" She folded the blanket back long enough to stretch out next to me and then covered herself up.

"Yeah," I mumbled, and I rubbed the sleep from my eyes. "I did."

Maylin sighed and propped her head on the heel of her palm, her elbow buried in the pillow. I thought of her life and how she did every single thing my parents wanted her to, though she did a bit of sneaking around too, like any college student. Andrew and Thomas had been little miniatures of my father. They still were, despite a few times of rocking the boat. I seemed to be the wild child, pushing back, making my own way. I wondered if Maylin was happy just doing what she was told or if she wanted to be free to make her own choices too. I wondered if I was making it harder for her now or if by my example of breaking free, she'd be able to choose boldness and carve her own way.

"What happened?" she asked me quietly, and I figured if I could hear them talking outside my room, there was a chance Mom was eavesdropping. The idea of their overhearing me made me feel so anxious, but I had to get this off my chest. It wasn't exactly how I wanted my parents to find out, but at least if Mom was listening in, I wouldn't have to see the initial shock and disappointment in her eyes.

I sighed hard and lowered my voice further, to almost a whisper. "Well, they said I'm anemic. They told Mom and Dad it's because of exhaustion."

"But?" she prompted, glancing at the door. With the light on in here, I couldn't see if there was a shadow on the door from the crack underneath.

"But I'm pregnant." My hand shot out to cover her mouth, and I raised my eyes in hopes she'd get the point. She started to squeal but silenced herself and nodded in understanding. Then I lowered my hand and closed my eyes. "And yes, before you ask, it's Dr. Thornton." I couldn't look her in the eye and admit that she'd gotten to me, but a dumb smile did stretch across my face.

"Oh, you little vixen!" Maylin pushed my shoulder playfully and then hissed, "Does he know?"

Sucking in a breath, I nodded, and then I slowly looked up at her. "He found out yesterday when I was in the ER, but then Mom and Dad showed up and he had to rush out. I don't even know what he really thinks about it and I'm terrified Dad is going to completely freak."

"Oh, he is." She raised one eyebrow and I moaned.

"Thanks for your kind sympathy and encouragement," I said sarcastically.

"Well, what did you think would happen? Why weren't you careful?" The tone she had was more of sisterly concern than a lecture, but the words still stung. We had been careful but not careful enough. And I hadn't thought about anything except my desire for him and how he was looking at me.

"Just tell me you're not disappointed in me too." My body felt like it'd been through a war. I was constantly nauseous, exhausted, achy, and my boobs hurt so bad as the hormones made them swell. I just needed some sort of ray of sunshine.

"Disappointed? Soph, you have just made me look like the poster child for perfection." She chuckled, but then rested her hand on my shoulder. "For real, though, I'm glad you broke out of your stodgy mold and did something fun for yourself. You deserve to be happy. I'm sorry it's going to come with such a huge weight of responsibility, but hopefully, that man helps you."

"Yeah," I mumbled, knowing Jack would definitely pull his weight. He loved Leah, and something told me when the shock of this wore off, he'd love my baby too. I just didn't know if it was the end of our relationship or the start of something amazing now. And since I didn't have my phone, there really was no way to find out.

"Hey, look at the bright side."

"What bright side?" I asked her, rolling my eyes.

"Now I can screw up a little more and still not be as bad as you." Maylin winked at me, and I chuckled. If the only thing to come of this with Mom and Dad was that Maylin had a lighter standard on her shoulders and they judged her a little less harshly, it was positive. I just wasn't sure I was going to live through the lectures when they figured out what was going on and were so crushed their perfect daughter had fallen from her pedestal.

"He's so perfect, May-May." I whimpered after I spoke, and she curled her arm under her head and rested fully on the pillow, listening to me. "We have so much in common, and he is smart and funny. Sure, he has a kid, but she's great too, and I think she likes me. And we can talk for hours without being bored of each other. We have the same interest and hobbies, and—"

"And it sounds like you're totally in love with him." She interrupted me, and it made me start crying again. I felt like I'd been crying for weeks now, every time I thought about how much I loved Jack and how much I wanted him to be my forever.

"Yes," I wailed, and she sighed.

"Does he know this? Are you guys serious about having something?" Her honest questions struck a chord with me. If Jack wasn't serious, he'd never have suggested going to HR. He'd have just broken it off with me. But just because he wanted me didn't mean he wanted the ready-made family.

"It's complicated," I told her, and that was the understatement of the year. "I just have to talk to him, but my phone is at work in my locker. They discharged me from the emergency room and I never got to go to the lounge to get it." I pouted out my bottom lip, and she nodded understandingly.

"Well, give yourself some time to think things through and try not to overthink. It will work itself out." Maylin patted my shoulder and rolled off the bed, almost taking the blanket with her. I gripped it and held it across my body as she turned to say, "Coming for dinner? Mom almost had it ready when I got here."

It'd been twenty minutes already, so dinner was probably done, but if I ate anything, I'd start upchucking again. I didn't need more questions. "No, I'm not hungry. Just tell them I have a headache and I'm going to sleep it off." And when I woke up, I was going to find a way to get to my locker and get my phone and call Jack. The fear of the unknown was killing me.

Maylin stood at the door and said, "Go easy on yourself, Sis. You're human." Then she walked out. I knew my secret was safe with her, but it couldn't stay a secret forever. I had to figure things out with Jack and I had to figure out how to tell my family. Before things got even worse.

28

JACK

I t was eight a.m. I'd been sleeping in the on-call room all night. Sophia hadn't called me, nor had anyone to say they needed me for help in surgery, but after the day I'd had and the revelation of being a father again, I was glad the work part was quiet. My sleep was fitful, filled with dreams of losing Leah, of Sophia collapsing and dying. I didn't feel rested. I felt like I could go back to sleep and rest for hours.

But I had to check in with Howard and see how things were going. He told me to call this afternoon, but in the chaos, I'd forgotten. It was late, far too late to call his office, but I had his personal number because we played golf from time to time when my schedule was lighter. So I dialed him and waited.

"Jack, how's it going? It's late." Howard was a very direct person, not the type to beat around the bush. I figured I had interrupted his family time or maybe his dinner. I didn't want to waste any more of his night than I needed to so I got right to the point.

"Howard, I have some news and I'd like some updates." I rubbed some sleep out of my eye as he spoke.

"Well, let's tackle the update first. Judge Greer won't allow Dana's suit to move forward for sole custody, but he may permit her to seek a new agreement after her relocation. It'd allow her to have Leah every week and you have her every weekend plus alternating holidays. You'd be hard pressed to find a better deal than that, though."

My heart sank at his news. I couldn't do that to Leah, because I knew damn well I had to be on call every other weekend. Right now, it worked out with Dana having Leah every other weekend while I had her on Wednesdays too.

"Well, that won't work for me." I felt frustrated and stubborn, but I had to do something.

"What's your news, then?" Howard asked, and I braced myself for his reaction to my surprise. I wasn't sure if it was good news as far as the custody hearing was concerned, but to me it was very good news.

"Well, I've been seeing someone and it turns out I'm going to be a father all over again. I'm just giving you a heads up because eventually, it's getting back to Dana, and I'm sure she'll throw a fit."

"I see." At first I thought Howard sounded like this was a horrible thing, but when he spoke again I felt relieved. "Well, congratulations, Dad. Next time you're in my office, let's smoke a cigar... In the meantime, that will actually play well for the judge. He'll see you bringing a new family aboard and see the stability. He'll see Leah as having a new sibling, and that will make him lean toward wanting to keep her closer to her family here in Denver. It might work in our favor."

The news was encouraging to me, but not enough to make me relax yet. I couldn't let Dana take my child away and move to another state. I knew it was the beginning of a slippery slope. Leah had to stay here. If not, I'd lose her for good.

"And what if I countersue? I want my daughter to be with me full time. I don't know anything about the men Dana's seeing and I don't trust them. Leah doesn't have anything good to say about them." I held my breath waiting for Howard to respond, and I loved his answer.

"We can do that. You'd have a good shot. Based on her lawyer's paperwork, I've noticed a few of the guys she's had in and out of that house are unsavory types. One of them has a criminal record. That's definitely not going to look good to a judge."

That answer both disgusted me and encouraged me at the same

time. "Good. Then go ahead and get the papers started. I want to countersue for sole custody. Leah belongs with me."

"No problem, Jack. I'll have them ready for you to sign first thing Monday morning." Howard excused himself to what sounded like his dinner being served, and I shoved my phone in my pocket.

It wasn't like Sophia to not call, but after the long day she'd had and feeling ill, she was probably resting. I stood and stretched, then headed out. My plan yesterday was to go to HR and discuss with someone there the situation and find out what to do. I hadn't intended to sleep so long, and I wasn't even on call last night. So, waking up in the hospital and needing a shower had been the last thing on my mind.

When I got to the HR office, there were only a few people on the clock. The redhead with a crooked nose who sat at the reception desk looked more like an administrator than a secretary, and I figured it was short staffed right now, it being the weekend. But I had questions with no answers and I wanted to put my mind at ease on a few things. I'd read the policy, but it was uncertain and left room for interpretation. If I had something more concrete to tell Sophia the next time we spoke, I'd feel better.

"Can I help you, honey?" the woman asked, and I wasn't even surprised to hear the nasally tone of her voice as she looked up at me.

"Uh, yeah… I'm here to discuss the non-fraternization policy with someone. Is there a rep I can speak with?" I wasn't sure who my rep was, but any of them would have access to the standard and be able to answer my questions.

"I'm it today, honey… We only staff a few people on the weekend." She took out a pair of glasses and slid them on, then used a finger on the frame to push them up the bridge of her nose. "What can I do for you? Is this a harassment thing?"

I shifted my weight from one foot to the other and stared at the split-pea-soup green color of the walls. Everything in this hospital was so ugly and mundane—like that wall color that was everywhere, except maternity.

"If a supervisor starts a relationship with one of his employees, how does HR handle that?" My questions had to remain very vague. Eventually, Sophia and I would fully come forward, but now that she had an added complication, I wanted to do things the best way possible for her. If I were able to move to a different department and shift her and Dr. Briggs over to one of the other surgeons on staff, it would be better for her. I just had to play my cards right.

"Well, that's tough to say. If they've been hiding a relationship for a while, likely, one of them would be fired, probably the supervisor if there was any indication it was motivated by their authority. But if you're talking a run-of-the-mill declaration of relationship, the employee would be reassigned to a different department and they'd be granted permission to have the relationship." She scrunched her nose and pushed her glasses up again. "Of course, it's up to the board to decide, not us in HR."

Taking my chances with the board didn't sound good at all. Sophia had fought her parents so hard to stay here, and if she got shifted around, I'd have done nothing but hurt her more, and just when she needed this job more than ever.

"And how long is 'a while'?" I asked.

"Oh, you know… a month or two." She winked at me and asked, "So, is there a relationship you'd like to declare? You should probably wait until Monday when your rep is here."

I took a step backward, already regretting coming here. If one or two months was the cut off for "a while" then Sophia and I were screwed. It had already been two full months and we were starting on our third. If she got pregnant that first time we had sex, which was the only time we'd been even slightly reckless, that meant anyone with a brain and an understanding of the female reproductive system would know it had been far too long.

"Not at this time," I told her, and I let myself out. So, coming clean to HR wasn't the best idea unless I put in a transfer request and made sure Sophia wasn't going to be affected. I could still help her with learning. I just wouldn't be the one to whom she reported. And it would mean the only thing I could do was give up my career trajectory. I'd be shuffled into diagnostics or internal medicine and be moved far away from surgery where I wanted to be.

But if it meant having her, I'd do it.

I just had to wait until Monday and hope she called me before then.

29

SOPHIA

Sunday morning, I managed to choke down some breakfast while Mom and Dad were out. I made myself a piece of toast and kept it dry, hoping it wouldn't upset my belly. Maylin was sleeping in, so I sat at the kitchen table alone, thinking of Jack. I'd had the nerve to go to the hospital last night and get my phone, but when I put my shoes on and walked out, Dad was in the living room. I thought he'd gone to bed. He asked me where I was going and I realized I was stuck unless he gave me permission to drive his car.

I didn't have the guts to ask, so I just sat on the front porch for a while and got some fresh air. When I noticed that he'd gone to bed, I did too, with a listless feeling about the future. Mom informed me earlier that they'd called the hospital on my behalf and told them I was taking a week off, which I very much was not taking a week off. I'd be there tomorrow morning one way or another, but it might require me using Maylin's Uber, if she let me.

Now, I just had to keep myself focused on not throwing up whatever I ate. I had yet to find anything my stomach accepted and I was hungrier than normal with a growing fetus in my womb. I was pleased when the first few bites didn't come up instantly, but after the very first sip of fruit juice, I was on my knees by the trash can. And I was still there when Mom and Dad came home.

Dad went to his office and never saw me, but Mom brought some fresh produce into the kitchen and met me on my knees, holding my hair back. She brought a paper towel for me to blow my nose and wipe my face, and while I was leaving the rest of my breakfast there, she rubbed my back and spoke softly to me.

"You know, Sophia. Dad and I were fools when we were younger." Her hand smoothed over my shirt in circles and I had no clue what she was talking about. "Andrew and Thomas were so young when I did my residency. It made things so difficult for me. But you know, young love is passionate and risky. You make choices you don't think about."

I felt another strong wave of vomit and tried to block her out. She picked a rather stupid time to be nostalgic about us as kids. I just wanted to eat without throwing up. I was losing weight as it was instead of gaining, and my body was weakened by the anemia. If I just kept throwing up my vitamins, they'd be pointless.

"And my goodness, the morning sickness I had too. I couldn't eat for weeks and when I did, the only thing my body let me really enjoy was waffles. I had to try to sneak in some vegetables through juices." She chuckled, and I started to get the feeling that she wasn't going to be shocked when I told her I was pregnant. I knew all this throwing up was too obvious.

"I drank spinach in my morning coffee." She laughed, and I sat back and took the paper towel from her hand. "Oh, that was so awful. But I made it through."

"Mom, what are you talking about?" I asked, trying to act really confused, but deep down, I knew it was too late. She'd figured it out somehow and I didn't have a leg to stand on. I sat on the floor by that trash can and blew my nose, waiting for the hammer to fall.

"Oh, Sophia, it's okay. I've known since that day at your apartment." She stood up and offered me her hand, and I took it. When I rose next to her, she hugged me.

"Known what?" I asked, because if she didn't say it first, I would be a fool to confess it.

"That you're pregnant, silly." Mom held me at arm's length, and while I saw the disappointment in her eyes, I saw more compassion and love than anything else. "And it's okay."

"My God, it was Maylin?" I said, suddenly feeling frustrated with my sister. If she so much as breathed a word to them about this, I'd never speak to her again.

"No," Mom said, shaking her head. "May-May only spoke with us last night because she was concerned with you. She cares, and she put us in our place." Mom chuckled again, and I raised my eyebrows. May put them in their place? "She told us if we judged you or lectured you for this that she'd stop coming home for holidays and visits." Mom gestured at the table. Sit?"

I walked to the table feeling stiff and scared. So Mom knew about the baby, and it sounded like Dad knew too. Why wasn't he in here lecturing me? Why had he not lectured me last night when I sat on the front porch for air? Why had they not woken me up last night at any point and told me how stupid I was?

I sank into the kitchen chair as Mom opened the fridge and started putting away the food she got. She left a few things on the counter, pulled out the blender, and made me a smoothie with a vanilla yogurt base, some spinach, bananas, strawberries, and a bit of the same juice I'd just been drinking. When she sat across from me and handed me the glass, I stared at the ugly green concoction with disgust.

"Drink it. I promise, it's good and it will stay down." I took a sip and realized the green was only because of the spinach, but she was right. It did taste good. Whether it stayed down was another thing.

"I don't know what to do, Mom." I sighed and had another drink. I knew what I needed to do, but facing Jack meant facing the uncertainty of the job, his reaction, my future... my vulnerable heart.

"I say you have to talk to Mr. Thornton about that." Her eyebrows rose and I felt my throat constrict.

"She told you it was Jack?"

Mom nodded and her expression darkened. "Dad has some things to say about that too, but remember, he's seven years older than me... So that works in your favor."

None of this felt right. I pinched my arm and it hurt and I winced. Mom chuckled and I shook my head. "I'm just trying to decide if this is a dream. Why are you being so nice?"

While I drank more of the smoothie, Mom replied, "Because I know what young love is. I know how it's easy to get carried away and be hasty. And I know how driven you are. I know you weighed the risk and consequences against the benefits, and if you think this Jack person is worth it, then I trust your judgment."

It was the first time my mother had ever said those words to me, and I was shocked. But I didn't have time to respond to her because Dad walked in with a scowl on his face and a stack of papers. He dropped them on the table in front of me and pursed his lips.

Mom kept smiling as she looked at me, then Dad, then the papers. I glanced down at them and it looked like a work contract from UCHealth. The state teaching hospital across town had rejected my applications before. Why would Dad have this now?

"I got you a spot with Dr. Chase Partners at the big hospital." His grunt of dissatisfaction was exactly what I expected, but he wasn't lecturing me at least. "You can start in two weeks. They know about your... They know the condition you have," he said, and he seemed very stiff.

I knew something like this for Dad was huge. His family worked in a completely different way. He didn't understand people who chose to have sex outside of marriage or young people who got pregnant. To him, that was putting the cart before the horse and a gross injustice to those young people's future. I knew he was probably disappointed, so I didn't understand why he'd still be helping me.

"Daddy... you didn't have to do this." I picked up the paper and set the glass to the side. Mom was right. The mixture was staying down. Finally, I was able to eat something and not throw it up.

"Yes, I did. It's what parents do. Their kid makes choices with bad consequences, and the parents help them make it right so it doesn't affect the rest of their lives. And this one," he said, tapping the paper, "is not optional. I already turned in your letter of resignation at Twin Peaks. Accept this as my final word." He folded his hands in front of himself, and I nodded.

I was gravely aware of how stern he was and that he meant what he said. He'd follow through, and that would be the end of his helping me if I rejected this offer. It made my heart feel both terrifyingly sober and so fully loved at the same time. I stared at the contract with tears in my eyes, but Dad wasn't done.

"And as for Dr. Thornton, I expect him to do the right thing." Dad's tone was very gruff now. I could see in his eyes how angry he was. Dad was so old-fashioned. He didn't understand that American men don't officially ask parents for permission to date daughters. He needed to loosen up, but just the fact that he had broached this topic without shouting made me thrilled.

"You want to meet Jack?" I asked timidly.

"I forbid you from seeing him again unless he comes to meet me face-to-face and is a man. Do you understand me? It's bad enough that he's ten years older than you." Mom reached over and touched Dad's hand, and he sucked in a breath and relaxed his shoulders. "But he got you pregnant at a time in your career that you should have been protected. He has to answer to me for that. And if he is man enough to do that, I will consider giving my blessing."

I leapt to my feet with joy and threw my arms around Dad's shoulders sobbing happy tears. "Oh, Daddy!" I kissed his face and squeezed him and he put his arms around me too. The paper in my hand got crinkled, and I knew he'd have to print a new one, but all of this had worked out so differently from what I expected. I'd have to thank Maylin for using all her "baby of the family" wiles on them.

"I love you, qiān jīn," he whispered.

"I love you too, baba," I told him, and then I raced into the living room, but when I realized I didn't have a car, I returned. "Baba, can I use your car? I need to go to the hospital and get my purse and phone. I need to call Jack."

Dad scowled but handed me his keys, and I squealed again and hugged him one last time. Then I ran to his car and climbed in. Jack was never going to believe how this all worked out. And I prayed to God—if there was a God—that he'd had time to think about the baby and was as happy as I was.

I didn't know what to do if he wasn't. That prayer was my only hope.

30

JACK

I held the phone to my ear not even believing what I just heard. Howard's voice keeps rattling off the facts, but I'm stuck on the one that just made my life so much easier.

"Wait just a second," I tell him, halting his gibberish. "Go back and say that again."

Howard chuckles and repeats what I couldn't believe the first time. "Dana has dropped the suit, Jack. It's the truth. She said she can't take Leah away from her friends and family and she believes Leah's better off with you."

I still couldn't believe it. This wasn't like Dana at all. Normally, she would use any excuse to make me look bad or hurt me, and she never once thought of what was best for Leah. "So you think she just realized she was going to lose and gave up?" I asked, and he didn't even have to agree with me because my gut told me I was right. But he did.

"Honestly, yes. I put that countersuit forward and the judge told her to cough up details about the men she was with. I think it scared her off. The good news is, she gets one weekend a month and every other holiday, and she has to provide transportation." Howard scoffed. We both knew it wouldn't happen. She'd leave and never look back, and for once, I didn't know if that was a bad thing. Leah would be heartbroken, but she'd be better off.

"Look, I gotta run, Howard. Just let me know when to come by and sign the papers. There's someone I need to talk to."

It was like life switched directions in a split second and things had finally started going my way. I was so happy with this turn of events, I was ready to begin submitting my resume to other hospitals and surgical centers in the city, just to make sure Sophia and I could be together. I knew how things were with her family and I needed to honor that.

"Sure thing, Jack. I'll shoot you a text when my secretary has them all typed up. Have a good evening." Howard hung up, and I shoved my phone into my pocket. The only thing on my mind was figuring out where Sophia was so I could talk to her. I assumed based on the nurse from the ER's statement that Sophia was with her parents. It would be challenging, but I could look up her personnel file and her emergency contact, which was likely her mother, and go from there.

I grabbed my keys and my jacket and rushed for the door, but as I opened it to dash out to my car, Sophia was there, almost bumping into me. I stopped dead in my tracks and braced her by a firm grip on each elbow so she didn't fall over.

"My God!" she gasped, and then she smiled.

"I'm so sorry. I almost ran you over. I was just coming to find you." I wanted nothing more than to take her into my arms and kiss her until her breath was gone, but she looked somewhat giddy, which wasn't at all the expression I expected.

"Jack, my gosh. I have so much to tell you." It looked like she'd been crying, but I gathered based on her happiness and the tone of her voice that they had been happy tears.

"Me too." I grinned at her and gestured at the still-open door. "Want to come in?"

"Of course," she said, wiping her tears away.

I followed her inside, unable to contain my excitement. I sat on the couch so close to her, our thighs were touching. She still seemed breathless, and the excitement was so difficult to contain, so I went first.

"Dana dropped her suit. She's still moving away, but she gave me sole custody of Leah. Do you know what this means?" I asked her, and as I did, I watched her eyes. Sophia was happy for me. I could see it in her expression. But she had her own news to share and I was being selfish.

"Jack, that's so incredible. I know how much you love your daughter—"

My hand shot out to her stomach and I said, "My children," cutting her off. The comment brought more tears to her eyes, which when she blinked went cascading down her cheeks.

"You're happy?" she asked in almost a whisper.

"I couldn't be happier, Sophia." I shook my head and pulled her into my arms where she wept quietly for a moment. "It wasn't in my plans, but the idea of you having my baby sounds like the perfect way to celebrate this moment."

She sniffled and held me and then sat back on the couch. "Jack... I think we should go to HR together now because—"

"Soph," I said, cutting her off. My chest tensed and I sighed. "If we go to HR, they're going to reassign you or even fire you. Mostly likely, you'll be terminated. We waited too long." I was talking, but it was like she wasn't listening. Her smile stayed plastered on her face and I was confused. "I'll have to apply to other places, or apply to move to a different department because... Why are you smiling?"

"Jack, I want to go to HR to resign my internship." She wrung her hands in her lap nervously, but the same plastic smile on her face remained.

"What? Why? You need that internship." I shook my head. I couldn't let her give up this position when I knew how much she depended on it, how much she needed to prove her worth to her family.

"Listen?" she said quietly, and she still kept smiling. Sophia reached out and took my hand and held it, and I tamped down my emotions for the moment to listen to her. "My parents know." Her eyebrows rose. "About us, the job, the baby."

My shoulders felt tense as she said that, but her smile didn't fade at all. I didn't understand. She was so worried about this before. How could she be so happy now?

"I don't get it."

"Jack, Mom figured it out. She said she knew a while ago… Don't ask me how. But they know." Her eyes clouded with some sadness. "Dad is upset, understandably. But he is willing to support us if you can go talk to him, man to man."

The dreaded "meet the parents" talk was something every young man got nervous about, but a man my age meeting a very strict man like Sophia's father sounded even worse. Maybe the horror stories about him were worse than I thought, considering he was willing to support us if I could man up and go chat with him. But after seeing Sophia wrestle with dread for months, I wasn't sure.

"And?" I asked her, sensing there was a catch.

"And nothing," she said, and her smile returned. "He got me a spot at UCHealth. I'll have a full five-year internship with one of their trauma surgeons, and you can keep working at Twin Peaks just like you are now."

She brought my hand to her lips and kissed my knuckles, and when she looked back up at me, I was speechless. For weeks, we were concerned about things that now had become completely irrelevant. Life had worked out in such a way that everything we feared was washed away in less than a moment, as if it never existed.

"What?" I asked, not believing what I was hearing for the second time today. It was like the fates had spoken and with a single breath had removed every obstacle to our happiness.

"You heard me… Now, tell me again how you want to be a father, because I've been so sick with worry that you aren't wanting another baby."

I pulled her onto my lap and kissed her hard, smashing her against my chest. The word relief didn't even begin to describe what I was feeling. It was like the weight of the world had been lifted and the joy of a thousand lifetimes had flooded my soul.

"I love you, Sophia, and I want this baby more than anything in the world." I gave her no chance to respond as I claimed her mouth in another scorching kiss.

Now if I could contain myself long enough to meet with her father and obtain his blessing for dating and someday marrying his daughter, the rest would all be downhill.

SOPHIA

"Baba," I said, frowning. From the moment we walked through the door, Dad had done nothing but grill Jack.

Mom had made a lasagna, and while I fully expected Thomas and Andrew to be here, Maylin too, none of them had come. Our traditional Sunday evening family meal was just the four of us, a little too intimate, if you ask me. I would've preferred the distraction of my siblings to help keep a buffer between Jack, who seemed calm and collected, and my father, who was anything but.

The deep creases in his forehead betrayed his frustrations, but more so, it was the overly strict tone of his voice. Dad was roughly fifteen years older than Jack but spoke to him like he was only a rebellious teenager, not the experienced and wise doctor who was pushing forty.

"Sophia," Mom said cautiously. Her eyes warned me not to get involved, and she put another soft, buttery breadstick on my plate.

My shoulders slumped and I knew she was right. This was between the two men I loved more than anything in the world, and they had to work it out. Jack and I had a few long conversations over the past twenty-four hours. I knew without a doubt that if my father refused to give his blessing, Jack would care for me. He had no intention of letting me flounder. I'd still get the new internship at UC, but I'd be on my own for rent, food, and transportation—which Jack said he was happy to provide.

"I am saying a man of your age should have been more astute. You put my daughter's career at risk, threw down hurdles on her path to success, jeopardized her ability to care for and provide for herself, and now look. She'll miss at least two solid months of her second year due to maternity leave." Dad spoke with his hands, dropping garlicky crumbs of breadstick on the table and his plate.

I could see the veins in his forehead bulging as he spoke, and his eyes were wide and wild. He was so passionate about this, it was hard not to feel how much he loved me. But this wasn't a pissing match, and Jack was so respectful. I laid my hand on his thigh beneath the table and squeezed it as he started to respond.

"With all due respect, Dr. Chen, your daughter is the most powerful and capable woman I have ever met." I watched my mom blush and hang her head at Jack's compliment directed at me. She clearly loved Jack already. "I am positive that you raised your daughter with enough brains and ability to move mountains. She'd have pushed me aside to have my job in less than a year."

Dad harrumphed and scowled, then continued his lecture, but I could see him cracking. Jack pouring on the praise about Dad's ability to parent was helping my father see that Jack really did respect me and him.

"Now what will she do? She has a delayed start on her new internship. She will miss two months of work. And she will be a single mother. This is unacceptable. My daughter has been disrespected. Her honor has been shamed. She gave herself to you with trust and you—"

"Qīn'ài de," Mom said, and Dad stopped speaking. His nostrils flared and he glared at Jack, but he set his breadstick down on the table at Mom's gentle words. The term of endearment had always been her way of reining him in when he was upset with one of us children. Now, she used it to remind him that he was being hard on Jack, who might very well become one of his extended children one day.

When Dad had been quiet for a moment, Mom looked at Jack and nodded, her smile so polite you'd have thought she was the one feeling guilty for the entire event. Dad was upset. I understood that, but Jack didn't deserve the reaming he was getting. I was the one who let him do those things to me—those amazing, wonderful things that made me feel so incredible. We made the choice together and I wouldn't let Dad pin it all on Jack.

"Baba, I love this man." I sighed. "One day, I hope you will see that even if we did things in the wrong order, in your opinion, that love is love, and we want you to see how our relationship is just as valid as yours and Mama's."

Jack reached under the table and took my hand in his and laced our fingers together, then lifted our clasped hands and rested them on the table. Dad seemed irritated and stared at our union but said nothing.

"Dr. Chen, you have no idea how deeply I respect your daughter, and even the fact that you're so upset right now. If this were my daughter, I'd be just as outraged. We both want what is best for Sophia now. I believe what's best for her is to continue working toward her full licensure and board certification. Not only is she a fantastic surgeon, but she also deserves to chase her dreams and have her career."

Jack looked at me with love in his eyes. "I don't want to trap her or make her feel like she has to depend on me, but I won't for a second let her fail. Anything she needs, I will provide. But I want to see her successful and independent too." I knew Jack's words weren't just to impress my father, but I knew how Dad felt. Jack was hitting the nail on the head.

"Hmm," Dad said grumpily.

"Baba," I moaned, and I tore my eyes off Jack to smile at my father's grumpy expression.

"This is really what you want?" he grumbled, and his eyebrows peaked in the center.

"Yes, Baba. I love Jack." I smiled sweetly and watched as his expression softened.

Dad wiped his mouth with his napkin and kept the grumpy scowl on his face, but the way his shoulders slumped slightly told me we'd won the war. And none too soon. I was growing nauseous after the tomato sauce in the lasagna. I glanced at Mom, who now sat with her chin erect and a soft smile on her face.

"Dr. Jack Thornton, my daughter's heart is not to be toyed with." Dad was calm now as he spoke, and he sat back in his seat, folding his hands over his rotund belly. "She will finish her studies. She will take a well-paying job here in Denver close to her family. You will not control her decisions or sway her opinions. You will treat her with respect as the woman she is, not a pawn to play with."

Shame washed over me as Dad lectured Jack like he was a bad person for even looking at me, but Jack took it in stride. I supposed it was just what men had to go through to earn their future father-in-law's respect, but I hated it.

"Sophia is free to do as she pleases, and you will give her that respect and love her. It isn't an option. You will cherish her for the treasure she is, and you will provide for her when she has lack. Do I make myself clear?" Dad squared his shoulders again, and I burst with joy at Jack's response.

"Dr. Chen, it will be my greatest honor in this life, and any in my future, to provide any and everything Sophia needs or desires." Jack's honest response touched me, and my eyes welled up.

"I can't believe he is so old," Dad mumbled to Mom, and I chuckled, then pulled Jack's cheek down to plant a soft kiss there.

Then I stood and walked to the other end of the table where Dad sat. He looked up at me, but I dropped to my knees and wrapped my arms around him, resting my head on his stomach. "Thank you, Baba, for trusting my heart. I won't let you down."

"Neither will I, sir." I heard Jack's voice but didn't realize he'd followed me until Dad reached up and shook his hand.

"Hmm," he said, grumbling again. Mom laughed this time, then pushed her chair back and stood.

"Who would like ice cream?" she asked, and I leapt to my feet.

"I'll help," I told her, knowing it was finally safe to leave Jack alone with Dad.

We had a ways to go to convince my father to celebrate with us, but he was finally at least willing to give us a shot. This ice cream was well deserved and worth all the frustration of the entire night. Jack was right. If we just faced things head on, they were easier to deal with. Now we only had to tell Leah. I felt like that part was going to go very well.

32

JACK

Leah crawled up into her bed and curled up. She had brushed her teeth and put her pajamas on by herself, and following dinner with Sophia, she requested a bedtime story, which Sophia dutifully read, complete with acting out the voices. Now, it was time for her to lie down and go to sleep, and this time when she begged Sophia to do it, I couldn't resist her. It was time to talk to my daughter about her new sibling on the way.

"Daddy, since I'm staying with you more now, does that mean I can have Sophia over for sleepovers like Mandy?" Leah's friend from school hadn't been able to do sleepovers at Dana's house, but at times I had allowed the girls to do them here. It warmed my heart to know how much Leah loved Sophia.

"I think we can arrange that, baby." I sat on the edge of her bed and Sophia knelt next to me, smiling.

"Leah, do you know what's more fun than sleepovers?" Sophia asked, and I narrowed my eyes.

We both agreed that after the drama of packing all of Leah's things and the squabbles I had with Dana, that Sophia should be the one to tell Leah about the baby. It'd been an emotional week for both of us, and I didn't want Leah to think I loved the new baby more than her.

We hadn't been able to bring everything from her mother's house due to the stench of cigarette smoke, and that left some hard feelings which made me feel guilty.

"I don't know. Nothing is more fun than a sleepover. That's why I like them, but now I live here, so it won't be as exciting. But I get to see Daddy every day now." I was certain that eventually, she'd miss her mother, but for now, Leah was adjusting quite well to her new living situation.

"Well, friends come and go, right? You have friends in school, and then summer break comes and you don't see them as much... Then back in school, you might have totally different friends in your class for next year." I understood where Sophia was going with this, and I loved how thoughtful she was to help Leah understand.

"Yeah, that's sad. But Mandy and me are friends forever. She even said so." Leah pulled the floral and plaid bedspread up over her shoulders and tucked it under her chin as she turned on her side. Her curls clung to the side of her face with light perspiration. I didn't know how she could cover up when it was so warm in here.

"Well, what if you had a built-in friend forever? One who never had to go home, who got to have sleepovers every single night, and who would play with you every day." Sophia's face lit up as she spoke, and her enthusiasm was infectious.

"Mandy can move in here too?" Leah asked, and I chuckled.

"No, baby. What Sophia is talking about is called a sibling." I smoothed her hair back and folded the covers down a bit so she wasn't so warm.

"Yeah, I'm talking about a little sister or brother to play with."

As Sophia said the words, Leah's face lit up. She grinned and looked up at me and said, "A baby?"

"Yes, a baby." I nodded at her and recognized the joy in her eyes. It was how I felt when Sophia first told me too. A new baby in this house meant lots of nights pacing the floor with a crying infant but eventually would be a toddler and then a playmate for Leah.

"But Mommy moved away," Leah said, confused.

"And Sophia is here now." I raised my eyebrows.

"And I'm going to have a baby. And that baby will be your little brother or sister." Sophia reached up and took my hand and said, "Because I love your daddy very much." Her eyes sparkled with emotion.

"Wait. Where do babies come from?" Leah asked, and that was the end of this conversation.

"I'll tell you another time." I chuckled, tousling her hair. "It's time to sleep now, but Sophia will be here when you wake up and you can talk all about the new baby then." I stood and helped Sophia to her feet.

We headed toward the door, but Leah's voice called to us. "Daddy, I love you... And I love you too, Sophia. And I love the new baby too."

"Goodnight, sweet girl," Sophia said, and I led her out, shutting the door behind us.

Sophia started to head to the living room, but I had other plans. It had been days since we were alone together, and we had yet to properly cement and celebrate the blessing her father had granted. I pulled her into my bedroom and locked the door so that Leah wouldn't inadvertently walk in on us if she got out of bed, then I pinned Sophia against my dresser and covered her mouth with mine.

"You know, I can't wait until your belly is huge and in the way, and I have to put you in all sorts of odd angles and positions just to fuck you." I kissed her again, and she smiled against my mouth.

"Oh, yeah? Who says I'm going to let you fuck me when my belly is huge and in the way?" She draped her arms around me, and I smoothed my hands along every curve of her body.

"Oh, I promised your father to meet every one of your needs, and I've heard that pregnant women get super horny. Plus, orgasm is the best way to prepare the body for labor and delivery." I guided her toward the bed as I peeled her shirt up over her head and tossed it. Then I unhooked her bra and let her tits bounce free.

"Oh, is it?" she purred, loosening my belt. "I think I'm only ten weeks right now. You have a long way to go before I need prepped for labor and delivery." She rose up and nipped my lip as she pushed my slacks down over my hips and then started on my buttons, but I pushed her on the bed and she bounced with a giggle.

"Well, we have months to practice then, don't we?" I hooked two fingers into the waistband of her leggings on each side of her hips and tugged, and the soft cotton fabric folded back on itself as I pulled it off her legs. She lay on the bed in front of me with her legs spread and touched herself as I shed my clothing.

"My fucking God, I can't wait to fill you up with my seed." I growled as I nestled between her knees and kissed her again. Condoms were the bane of my existence, and knowing she was mine and she was already pregnant meant this would be incredible sex.

"No mess unless you make me come at least twice first." Sophia's playful tone made me grin as I sucked a nipple into my mouth and bit down. She hissed, "Jack," and rested her hands on my shoulders, and I sucked harder.

"Am I making you horny, Dr. Chen?" I purred, stroking her wet folds with my fingers, and she moaned.

"God, yes," she moaned, arching her hips up into my touch. "Please don't take all day."

"We have as much time as we want," I said, teasing a finger into her soaked entrance, eliciting a gasp from her. "Maybe after this, we'll take a nap, and I can fuck your brains out again." I removed my finger and rubbed it on her clit, circling the swollen nub once, twice, before plunging two fingers into her hot depths and curling them inside her with a groan.

"Jack... God, Jack, your fingers... I want more." She moaned, squirming under my touch. I leaned down and licked her nipple, sucking it hard.

"You'll get more," I promised as I continued to thrust my fingers into her. She moaned and moaned, arching her hips upward to buck against me. I wanted to taste her sweetness, savor the moment, suck every last drop of moisture from her pleasure zones until she was screaming my name.

Slowly, I backed down the bed, kissing a trail of fire over her tits and stomach until my mouth stopped at her pulsing valley. Her pussy clenched as I blew a hot breath across it, and her fingers tangled in my hair.

"Jack," she panted, her hips twitching as I blew on her clit again. "God, Jack."

"That's right, baby," I soothed as I teased her fleshy little nub with my tongue, swirling it around and around. Her juices were intoxicating, and I couldn't get enough of her taste.

"Fuck, more... harder," she moaned. I gave her what she wanted, sucking on her swollen clit while my fingers worked inside her. My free hand squeezed one of her breasts roughly, twisting the nipple between my fingers, and she cried out.

"Oh, fuck! Yes!" she moaned as her climax hit her like a freight train. Her juices flowed onto my chin and down to her thighs, and I lapped up every drop as she shuddered and bucked against my mouth.

"That's right, baby, come for me," I growled, and she moaned again. My cock throbbed impatiently against my stomach, ready to claim her. I removed my fingers and crawled up to claim her mouth in a fierce kiss as her orgasm subsided. She spread her legs, welcoming my hips between her thighs. As I ground against her, my dick slid through her moisture and she bit my lower lip.

"Now," she panted, and I obliged, plunging inside her wet heat. "Fuck me, Jack."

Sophia's walls clenched around me and I groaned. "I love the way you tighten around me." I pulled almost all the way out before slamming back in, and she moaned loudly as I found her G-spot again and again. Her fingernails dug into my back as I set a hard, fast pace, pounding into her until she came again with a cry. "Damn it, Jack," she whimpered from the intensity of her climax.

"I'm not finished yet," I growled between clenched teeth, picking up the pace. My body coiled tighter and tighter as pleasure unfurled deep inside me, threatening to explode out of my skin. The head of my cock throbbed with every thrust, demanding my release. I couldn't hold back any longer, and with a growl that was part animal, I unloaded inside her, white-hot pleasure tearing through me as I spilled my seed deep in her pussy. My balls throbbed, the pressure so much I thought my brain would explode, then so glorious a release I felt like I could pass out and melt into the sheets.

"Oh, fuck." I panted as I collapsed on top of her, my cock twitching inside her.

"I love you," she whispered in my ear, and I smiled as I rolled off to the side, taking her with me.

"I love you too, Sophia." I kissed her temple, plucking sweaty strands of her dark hair from her skin and curling them around her ear. "And I can't wait to do this every day for the rest of my life." In a moment of spontaneity, I said, "Move in with me. Just stay here. Let me get rid of that tiny apartment and take care of you."

"Oh, Jack," she said happily. "We just convinced Dad to give us his blessing. He's not going to go for that so soon..." She smiled thoughtfully. "But I'd love to have as many sleepovers a week as possible." She winked, and I knew she and I were on the same page.

Kissing her hard again, I growled, "Now give me fifteen minutes and we can go again. I can't get enough of your body."

Sophia snickered and pushed me away. "Let me pee," she said, and she rolled out of bed.

When all of this started, I wasn't sure what to think of it. All I knew back then was that I was infatuated with her mind and her beauty. Now I was helplessly in love. I never thought there'd be another woman who could tame the beast inside me, but there she was in all the glorious wisdom and gorgeous curves, and I couldn't be happier.

33

EPILOGUE: SOPHIA

I looked up at Jack in so much pain I thought I'd split in two. Three hours of this and no one had brought me the damn epidural I'd begged for. Now the doctor between my legs was telling me it was time to push, and I wasn't ready.

"No," I whined, tossing my head back. With my feet in the air like this, how was I supposed to do anything?

"You've got this, Soph. Now take a deep breath and bear down. I'm here. You can do it." Jack gripped my hand, and I wished I were strong enough to crush it. This pain was the worst thing I had ever experienced and I was over it.

"It fucking hurts!" I shouted, but I knew the only way out was to do what he said.

"Come on, baby. Just a few more pushes and we meet our little guy —or girl." Jack kissed my forehead as I sucked in a hard breath.

My body was worn out. I really didn't have it in me at all, but I bore down and gritted my teeth, focusing all my pressure in my bottom just the way the doctor coached. The pain was searing, and despite trying to hold my breath, I screamed out in pain again. Jack was there, whispering in my ear, trying to encourage me.

Ten more minutes of pushing and all I could think was if this kid didn't come out of me soon, I was going to pass out. But with one final push, I felt relief. I collapsed back onto the bed, and Jack wept over me, kissing my forehead. I couldn't see what was going on with my eyes shut from exertion and exhaustion, but I felt them lay something on my chest. I opened my eyes to see my perfect little boy just as he sucked in a breath and let out a tiny wail.

"A boy, baby. You gave me a boy." Jack's tears were large and streaming down his cheeks. I'd never seen him cry, and I'd never seen him so happy.

I stared at the angry face of my crying newborn, still coated in white vernix from birth, and I was already in love. "Jack Junior, I'm your mommy," I said as I started to cry too. Jack and I had picked out the name just in case. We hadn't discovered the sex before now, so this was a complete surprise.

"Jack Junior. I love that so much." Jack used the corner of the blanket they wrapped the baby in to wipe away some of the vernix from his forehead, then kissed him.

We spent the next hour bonding, cleaning Jack Jr., and letting the doctor and nurses get his stats. Six pounds, twelve ounces, nineteen and three-quarter-inches long. He was a tiny baby boy, and I was glad he wasn't larger. The pain of a tiny baby was bad enough.

"I want to go get Leah. Is that okay?" Jack hovered over me, and I nodded. The nurses were busy wiping Jack Jr. clean and swaddling him. I wanted to try nursing, and I knew Leah sat in the family waiting room with my parents, who'd also come to the hospital when we called to let them know I was in labor.

"Sure, but I'm so bushed. I'd like to nap for a bit before the whole family comes back. Tell them?" I asked him, and he pecked me on the cheek.

"Of course. I won't be long."

Jack rushed out and I lay back in bed and rested my eyes until the nurses brought me the baby. I cradled him, thankful that I was done with pregnancy for a while. I was also thankful that the back pain and horrible morning sickness would be over now too, though sleepless nights were ahead.

When the door popped open, Leah tiptoed in as if she would disrupt me. It was sweet that she was being quiet, though I knew first-hand from staying with Jack so much over the past few months just how rowdy she could be. Adjusting to a new baby in the house wouldn't be easy for anyone, but I was glad she was here to greet him on his first day in the world.

"Baby Jack-Jack!" Leah tried to crawl onto the bed, but Jack picked her up and held her over me so she could see her little brother. "Oh, he's so tiny!" She tried to whisper out a squeal, but it came out a little louder than intended. Her eyebrows shot up and she covered her mouth. "Sorry."

"It's okay, baby girl. You'll be surprised how loud Jack-Jack will be when he gets a bit older." Jack kissed her cheek, and she reached down to touch his check softly.

"He's so cute."

"Yes, he is. He's tiny too, so you have to be very gentle." I already felt protective of him, but it wasn't a new feeling for me. I'd felt protective and loving over Leah too. The past several months of her adjusting to a mother who just abandoned her had been challenging at times, and she had bonded to me almost immediately. I loved being a mother figure to her, and I knew how much she loved having me around.

"Will he call you Mommy?" she asked, "Or Sophia?" Her nose scrunched up, and she looked back at her father. Jack hoisted her to his hip and held on around her waist. She hugged him around his neck, and I felt my heart grow heavy. She didn't understand things, and it wasn't really my place to step in. Leah had a mother, even if that woman didn't want her anymore.

"Baby, Jack-Jack will call Sophia Mommy because she's his mommy." Jack pushed a curl out of her face, and she looked down at me.

"But I call her Sophia, and Mommy isn't here now." She shrugged, and I gave Jack a pleading look.

We had never spoken about this before and I didn't want to cross any lines, but in my heart, I wanted this little girl to never have to feel lesser than her brother or be jealous of the love Jack and I had for him. A child should never have to go through the pain of losing a parent, and while I was no replacement, I could be a surrogate.

"Leah," I said softly, "would you like to call me Mommy too?" I raised my eyebrows as Jack glanced at me with such emotion in his eyes I thought he might cry. "You don't have to. But you can if you want. I know I'm not your mommy, but I love taking care of you."

Leah looked up at Jack and shrugged both shoulders again, then turned back to me. "Yes," she said resolutely, and then gave Jack a smack on the lips. "Mommy and Daddy." Leah grinned happily and then sighed exasperatedly. "When do I get to hold Jack-Jack?"

She cocked her head at Jack, who chuckled and set her down. "Alright, big sister, you can hold him for five minutes, then Mommy has to rest. She's very tired today. And you can play with *wàigōng* and *wàipó* for a while." He took Jack Jr. from my arms after pronouncing the Mandarin names so horribly I had to snicker.

"What does that mean?" Leah climbed onto the pull-out sofa with her nose scrunched up again. I was thankful that Jack was trying to learn my father's language to prove to him that we both took the culture seriously, but he didn't have to try so hard.

"It means, Grandma and Grandpa, remember?" I coached, reinforcing Jack's lead. I'd never correct him, but I'd definitely communicate that my parents were totally okay with Leah calling them any term of endearment she felt comfortable with.

"Oh, Nana and Pop-Pop!" She grinned. "Yes. I like them."

I watched her hold our little boy and yawned, feeling sleep tugging at my eyes. I barely made it a full ten minutes before my body gave up the fight. I laid my head back and dozed, dreaming of bringing Jack Jr. home to a loving house with Jack and Leah by my side. I dreamed he proposed and we had a traditional wedding, though Dad insisted on the red dress, and then I dreamed he walked me down the aisle and gave me to Jack forever.

My heart was full.

After almost a full year of ups and downs, some complications during pregnancy, and more than enough vomiting to last me a lifetime, my son was here. Jack and I were basically under the same roof, and I'd found a receipt from a jewelry store that Jack didn't know I'd seen. It made me giddy thinking that any day, he'd propose to me and our family would be complete. Things always had a way of working out, even if in the beginning they didn't seem that way.

For now I needed rest. Because when *wàigōng* and *wàipó* came to visit baby Jack, there would be enough noise to bring the house down. And Maylin, Andrew, and Thomas—with his new wife—wouldn't be far behind.

Made in the USA
Monee, IL
13 February 2025

12106673R10111